EDGE'S PUNISHMENT

With his free hand Clyde began to slap Edge's pain-weary face with the palm and then the back of the knuckles. He slammed hard enough to knock the head from side to side within the limits imposed by the hand grasping the hair.

"Findin' out what it's like to be on the receivin' end now, ain't you, mister? You ain't so friggin' tough without some skinny, titless woman to back you with a gun. We're givin' the orders now. And we're givin' them to a lousy Mex greaser who ain't in no position to argue."

Clyde gave up on the slapping and folded the punishing hand into a fist again. He began to land short, jabbing punches against Edge's nose, causing a steady flow of blood to run from both nostrils.

Edge was too engulfed by the depthless ocean of hatred to be aware of this. He could hear what was being said to him. He was able to see everything that was directly in front of him. He felt each blow that landed against him.

Each and every part of what he heard, saw, and felt provided fresh fuel for the hatred that somehow acted to insulate him from the full force of his punishment.

THE EDGE SERIES:

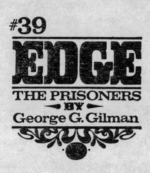

#39

EDGE

THE PRISONERS

BY

George G. Gilman

PINNACLE BOOKS   NEW YORK

EDGE #39: THE PRISONERS

Copyright © 1981 by George G. Gilman

Pinnacle Book first published in Great Britain by New English Library Limited in 1981.

First printing, April 1982

ISBN: 0-523-41450-1

Cover illustration by Bruce Minney

Printed in the United States of America

PINNACLE BOOKS, INC.
1430 Broadway
New York, New York 10018

For J.H., who keeps the chuck wagon supplied and rolling

THE PRISONERS

Chapter One

Joe Straw glimpsed the man riding slowly across the slope below the jagged ridge to the west and reined his own mount to a halt on the open trail. As the dust raised by the wearily moving hooves of Straw's gray gelding settled back on the hard-packed ground behind him, there were just two sounds to be heard in this arid piece of country among the eastern peaks of Arizona Territory's Santa Rosa Mountains: the breathing of the fatigued horse and frightened man seated astride.

On the high ground ahead and to the left of Straw, perhaps a half mile away, the man who had triggered the fear in him was no longer in sight. He had ridden his black mount into the cover of a line of scattered boulders from which he should have emerged less than a minute after going from sight.

But a minute and a half crawled into history and then the sweat of the mid-afternoon heat which clung to Straw's filthy flesh was augmented by the larger, tackier, more draining beads of salt moisture which oozed from his pores by heightening fear.

1

It was not Joe Straw's fault that his body smelled rancid with accumulated dirt. It was on account of his treatment by that bastard John Hackman, sheriff of Crater, Territory of Colorado.

Was it that hard-nosed lawman up there among the boulders pretending not to have seen his escaped prisoner and hoping Straw did not see him? Now, he was undercover, waiting for the man on the open trail to ride within effective rifle range.

Straw fought against the rising fear and the threat of panicked action that accompanied it. Because he was half Comanche, it was not as difficult to accomplish as it would be for most wholly white men.

He sat his horse in a relaxed attitude like a man simply taking a rest in the saddle and glanced about him in a manner of idle curiosity.

The half-breed was a handsome man in his twenty-ninth year with the curly red hair and flashing green eyes of his Irish father and the bone structure and skin coloration of the Comanche squaw the Irishman raped. He was six-feet tall and built on, slender lines, his litheness compensating for what he lacked in sheer brute strength.

Throughout his life, initially with his outcast mother and then as a complete loner after he sold her into slavery in Mexico, he had never attempted to conceal what he was in terms of his heritage. He chose to dress in a mixture of the Indian and the white man's styles. On this blisteringly hot day he wore a derby hat, a beaded waistcoat and highly decorated choker and tie that left his arms and belly bare, blue denim pants, and high-

2

heeled riding boots with work spurs, the entire outfit the worse for long wear.

The gunbelt buckled around his waist was relatively new, the loose hanging holster was empty. He did carry a weapon, a throwing knife in a sheath stitched to the inside of his pants waistband at the small of his back, the jutting handle concealed by his loosely fitting waistcoat.

Such a weapon was of no use in this situation and the reason he scoured his surroundings so intently from behind a shield of apparent nonchalance was to seek a way to alter the circumstances. Either get close enough to the man on the ridge to use the knife againt him or to escape without running the risk of pursuit across open country with a near exhausted horse under him. A killing shot or recapture would be inevitable.

The chances of accomplishing either aim looked slender. The stage trail ran along the bottom land of a broad valley, barren but for a few clumps of desert vegetation and sparsely featured in the immediate area with the kind of broken rocky terrain where the man on the ridge was concealed. The trail was closer to the western slope than the east and ran ahead of him as straight as a prairie railroad until it disappeared into the slick looking heat shimmer.

The head of the valley was behind him, the ground sloping gently upwards. Straw realized that to retreat in this direction was the only course open. He would have to ride across a quartermile of featureless terrain, but he knew that beyond the ridge where the trail curved there was another valley angling between the northeast and southwest completely devoid of vegetation, but filled with countless pockets of cover among a petrified sea of crumbling rocks resulting from some primeval movement of the earth.

So if he could spur his weary horse to cover the open ground fast enough, to stay out of range of a well placed rifle shot until he was beyond the crest of the rise, he would have a chance of retaining his freedom, maybe to guarantee it if John Hackman got careless and allowed himself to be lured into a trap.

A nagging doubt held Joe Straw where he was for several seconds. The valley behind him had provided the ideal opportunity for the lawman to swing wide and get ahead of his escaped prisoner. Why had he chosen to do this, though? It was also the perfect terrain for Hackman to set up the kind of dry-gulching trap which Straw was considering from behind, ahead, or to either side.

So why had he been riding across the open slope? Because he did not realize that he was ahead of his quarry until he saw that he was and had the good fortune to have cover close at hand?

Straw spat a globule of saliva down at the trail and set his well sculptured features into an irritable scowl. Whether the man on the ridge was John Hackman or not, he had seen the other lone rider on the trail. The fact that he was in hiding did not bode well for Joe Straw. To carry his thinking on the subject beyond this was futile.

So he thudded his spurs into the sweatlathered flanks of the gelding and voiced a shrill curse as he jerked the reins to the side.

The horse snorted his distress, but responded to the commands, brought up his head, wheeled into a tight turn, and began to beat at the sloping ground with galloping hooves.

Over the first twenty yards or so, Straw kept his head craned to the side, peering back over his right shoulder. He didn't see the slightest sign of movement among the jagged boulders where he knew the man was.

Then his horse stumbled, incapable of maintaining the speed the rider demanded. Straw used the spurs and reins viciously to steer his mount out of the threatened fall so that pain rather than exhaustion became the dominant sensation in every fiber of the gelding's being. His equine brain decided that speed provided the only means to escape further ill treatment.

Astride his black mare in a depression behind the boulders on the ridge, the man called Edge growled, "Toss the bastard out of the saddle, you crazy animal."

But it was a bullet that unseated Joe Straw, blasting into the front of his left upper arm and tearing free at the back in a welter of blood and remnants of flesh as the half-breed Comanche snatched another glance over his right shoulder.

He vented a shriek of alarm as the impact of the lead spun him into a half turn. The sound took on the tone of mixed fear and anger when he glimpsed the man who fired the shot.

With the vicious bite of the spade no longer digging into his tongue and the constant stab of the spur rowels momentarily ceasing their punishment of his bleeding flanks, the gelding submitted to the irresistible urge to slow from the gruelling gallop. All four of his legs were simultaneously drained of strength, splaying out to the sides so

5

that the animal came to a slithering halt on his belly. The sudden loss of momentum lifted the rider off his back and pitched him over his violently shaking head.

A great cloud of fine white dust exploded up from the trail and the wounded Joe Straw was hurled out of its midst, thudding to the hard ground twenty feet ahead of where the horse struggled for several seconds to rise. A trailing hindleg was broken, the jagged bone jutting through a blood soaked hole in his coat. He gave up the struggle and lay almost as still as the unseated rider.

The short and solidly-built, twenty-five year old lawman from Crater, Colorado was also unmoving for long moments. Sitting erect in the saddle on his black gelding, the Winchester rifle still to his shoulder, he aimed rock steady at Straw after tracking his involuntary plunge through the air.

Then, certain the man crumpled on the ground was unconscious or dead, he lowered the rifle and booted it. He clucked his horse into an easy walk from the high point of the trail where it ran from one valley into the other.

There was a bewildered expression on his square-shaped, ruggedly-hewn, heavily-bristled face as he made a rapid survey of the valley ahead and then returned his unblinking gaze to Joe Straw who was not dead. He was close enough to see his chest rising and falling. The dust in which the side of his face lay was gently stirred by his breathing.

What puzzled the black-clad man with a six-pointed star pinned to his left shirt pocket was the reason for the Comanche half-breed's frenetic

6

race up the slope, backtracking on a trail he had to know was being followed. There was nothing out along this virtually featureless valley that hinted of danger.

Hackman ignored the weak struggles and faint sounds made by the suffering horse as he came to where Straw lay and swung out of his saddle. Then he rasped the back of his hand over his bristled jaw and grunted his satisfaction with a thought that occurred to him.

Straw had been hallucinating. It had been day and a half since the breed made his sneaky escape, and in all that time he could not have eaten or drunk anything. During the heat of the day and the coolness of the night, he had not rested. Weary, hungry, and thirsty, his mind had played a trick on him. Maybe he had seen the heat shimmer as being closer than it was and in it he glimpsed some brand of mirage that was more frightening than the prospect of turning to race back into the gunsights of the lawman hunting him. A lawman whom he knew would regard his death as a failure desperately wanted to recapture him and bring him to Crater.

Hackman drew a knife from the opposite side of his gunbelt from where the holstered Remington was hung, and without shifting his cold-eyed gaze from Straw, he cut a length from a front rigging tie of his saddle.

"You won't get another chance to run out on me, you murderin' sonofabitch," he snarled as he moved closer to Straw and squatted at his side.

The man's bullet-holed left arm was already behind his back. Hackman had to roll the limp form over on to his belly to reach for and bring the

7

right arm to where he could lash the wrists together.

Another sound apart from the breathing of the two men and two horses reached the Crater sheriff's ears. He snapped his head up to look across the angle where the southern and western slopes of the head of the valley merged to see that the sound was made by a slowly moving horse and rider coming toward him.

"So it wasn't no imaginary . . ." Hackman began to rasp as beads of sweat dripped from his eyebrows to blur his vision.

Joe Straw, drawing upon his final reserve of strength, made his move. He flung himself over on his back, a groan of pain venting from his gritted teeth as his weight was momentarily on his injured arm. Then he crashed into the squatting lawman and sent him sprawling on his back with a bellow of rage and alarm.

The half-breed Comanche did feel eerily lightheaded now so it seemed to his pain wracked mind that his movements and Hackman's counters were enacted in slow motion.

The right hand the sheriff had so obligingly placed close to the sheathed knife clawed at the back of the waistcoat, fisted around the knife, and drew it.

Dust floated up around Hackman at his back, and the back of his head crashed against the ground.

Straw rose on one knee and forced himself into a turn between the splayed feet of the lawman.

Hackman struggled to fold his back up from the ground and snatched for the Remington in the holster.

8

Straw stretched out his good arm but had no strength to raise it. The glinting blade that seemed to be growing out of his hand clenched into a fist hovered for part of a second. He saw each individual bristle on Hackman's face and read the despair in his dark eyes.

The hoofbeats which had distracted the sheriff and given Straw the opportunity to make this move were louder now, but not approaching the scene of the death struggle at a faster pace.

The Remington was clear of the holster and Hackman was halfway up into a sitting posture. One of his booted feet was being drawn back and Straw knew the intention.

The sheriff did not want to kill him unless it was essential to his own survival so he was planning to lash a kick at his chest—to send him tumbling over backwards, with a stunning blow that would make it impossible for him to throw the knife with killing power.

Straw spat out the Comanche word for *die* and fell forward. He experienced excruciating agony as he fended off the kick with his injured arm, but he managed to keep his good arm ramrod stiff until his knife penetrated Hackman's shirt, undershirt, and finally his skin to delve deep into the boneless flesh of his belly.

The lawman gasped at the stabbing impact of the blade. He struggled to sit up, but then vented the shrillest of screams as his back slammed down to the ground and his arms flung wide to the side, the Remington sailing clear of his right hand to thud to the dust off the trail. His reaction, as Straw, the heel of his hand hard against the other man's shirt front, flicked his wrist without loosen-

9

ing his grip on the handle of the knife caused the inch-wide blade to turn viciously within the entrails of the Crater sheriff.

Hackman's entire body was convulsed by the bolt of agony that exploded at the source of the injury and was transmitted to every nerve ending.

Straw, on the brink of unconsciousness, mistook this violent movement for a counterattack, released his grip on the knife, and forced himself to roll clear of the flailing limbs of the screaming man.

For seconds both men were totally detached from their surroundings, each in a private world of pain and the fear of death. One was quaking from head to toe and the other struggling desperately to suck in and expel the hot, dusty air.

Then they both became aware of being shaded from the sun and they forced their eyes open to see what it was that towered between them and the sky. Each recalled when he first saw the stranger who was the cause of this explosion of violence.

"You fellers mind if I take a hand in this?" Edge asked flatly as he slid a Winchester out of his forward hung rifle boot.

"You ain't gonna kill us?" John Hackman rasped through chattering teeth.

"I ought to put a bullet in him," Edge answered, with a glinting glance at Joe Straw as he pumped the lever action of the repeater to eject a spent shell and jack a fresh one into the breech.

Through his pain and fear, the half breed Comanche had what was required to direct a challenging glower up at the mounted man. "Why

10

me, man? You and me don't know each other, do we?"

"I know you're the kind that should never be allowed to ride a horse, feller."

Edge raised the rifle stock to his shoulder, raked the barrel around, angled it down, and triggered a bullet cleanly between the agony-filled eyes of the crippled horse.

Straw almost managed a grin as he watched the impassive man in the saddle slide the Winchester back into his boot. "I knowed you was kiddin', man."

"Maybe if I was a female, feller."

"What you talkin' about?"

Edge climbed down from the saddle. "A feller mistreats a horse the way you do sure does get my goat."

Chapter Two

The half-breed Comanche watched the half-breed Mexican cross to where John Hackman was sprawled and attempt to will renewed strength back into his drained and punished body.

The man he surveyed was big—three inches taller than six feet and weighing close to two hundred pounds. He was built on lean lines with no surplus fat on his frame and dressed Western trail riding style in a gray Stetson with a low crown and wide brim, blue denim shirt and pants, single holstered gunbelt and spurless riding boots. This outfit was dusty and sweat stained from a long ride, but had not lost the stiffness of new fabric and leather.

Of older origin was the thong threaded with dull-colored beads that encircled his neck, which appeared to be the man's sole adornment in his otherwise entirely practical style of garb. Joe Straw had no way of knowing that attached to the beaded thong at the nape of Edge's neck was a leather pouch which hung down inside his shirt which held an open straight razor.

Unlike Straw, Edge did not go to great lengths

13

to advertise the mixture of bloods which coursed his veins. He adopted an underplayed Mexican-style moustache which was barely distinguishable from the matting of bristles that cloaked the flesh of his lower face and neck. Even without this, the structure and coloration of the features of his lean face provided enough clues to his mixed parentage.

He had eyes of ice blue in permanently narrowed sockets under hooded lids, an aquiline nose with flared nostrils, high cheekbones from which the skin was stretched taut to the firm jawline, and a straight, thin-lipped mouth.

His complexion was stained to a dark brown hue from exposure to the extremes of the elements and the hair that framed this face was jet black and worn long enough to brush his shoulders.

A handsome face in the rugged cut of the features, Straw allowed, and yet somehow it was ugly because of the latent cruelty of the man suggested by the thin mouthline and the slitted, hard glinting eyes. The half-breed Comanche found it difficult to guess the age of the tall, lean man who now looked down at the doomed John Hackman. The skin of his face was inscribed with countless lines that were not all put there by the passage of time. Maybe they were, but it was the depth of them that detailed the harshness of time he had lived.

Not that it mattered to Joe Straw. He merely studied the stranger as a mental exercise—a solid piece of reality to fasten his awareness on. Otherwise he might allow his eyes to close and submit to the demands of his pain and exhaustion and drift into a sleep close to unconsciousness.

14

The dying sheriff looked up at Edge, but saw him less clearly for his eyes were blurred with tears which he was unable to fist out of them. In the wake of searing agony had come a paralyzing numbness that made it impossible for him to move any muscles below his neck.

"Who are you?" he asked, speaking in a hoarse whisper.

Edge dropped onto his haunches and at close quarters confirmed his guess that the knife which was buried to the hilt in the center of all the bloodstain, which was already drying on the shirt of the lawman. To withdraw the blade from the depths of the belly would hasten death.

"Name's Edge, feller. Only way I can help you is to finish you the same way as the horse." He read the two words engraved on the tin star:

CRATER

COLORADO

"Let the bastard suffer, man," Straw growled. "You saw the way he blasted at me when I didn't have no chance to defend myself."

"Guess that's what you'll do, Edge," Hackman forced out through his clenched teeth.

"Why's that?"

The lawman blinked several times attempting to clear his vision of the tears, but it failed and he continued to see the squatting man as little more than a dark silhouette against the dazzlingly bright sky.

"I ain't seein' so good. You talk like a white man, but you look like some kinda Indian like Straw."

"Pa was Mexican, feller. My Ma was from Northern Europe. I figured myself to be an Ameri-

15

can. Forty next birthday and riding from Tucson to wherever this trail takes me." He took the makings from a shirt pocket and began to roll a cigarette. "But why should my life story interest a lawman a lot of miles away from home, feller? Especially one who ain't got too long to live what's left of his?"

"I know that sure enough, mister. But this weepin' that makes it hard for me to see ain't cause I know I'm ready to die. It's cause I'm gonna die before I bring Joe Straw back to Crater."

Edge struck a match on the butt of his holstered Frontier Colt and lit the cigarette. "Figure there never was anybody went to the grave happy he did everything he wanted."

Hackman acknowledged that he would not see clearly again and he squeezed his eyes tightly closed. "Want you to know somethin', mister?"

"Sure."

"I don't blame you for what happened."

"Wasn't planning to lose any sleep over it, feller."

"I'd like to thank you for givin' me the chance to stick him, man," Straw added, his voice stronger now.

Edge shifted his impassive gaze from the bloodless face of the lawman and fixed it on the half smiling features of the half-breed Comanche.

"I'd like for you to keep your mouth shut," he said evenly.

Straw's expression altered to a glower. "What's Hackman to you, man?"

"Somebody who wanted something real bad

and ain't going to get it," Edge replied to the man, but returned his attention to the other.

"The stage coach line put up a reward, mister," the lawman croaked. "One thousand lousy dollars."

"Which you as a sheriff ain't in line for?"

"If I had ten times that much, I'd pay it to see Straw strung up in Crater."

"Personal, uh?"

"My old man was drivin' the Denver to Crater stretch, mister. Straw blasted his head off with a shotgun."

"The crazy old timer tried to kill me!" Straw countered. "It was him or me, for frig sake! I didn't have to hurt no one else aboard the stage!"

Edge pursed his lips and allowed a sigh to trickle out with tobacco smoke as he unfolded to his full height. Then he stepped over the unmoving form of the dying sheriff.

With a wail of fear, Straw tried to roll away from the advancing man with a cigarette angled from a corner of his mouth.

Hackman wrenched his head to the side and snapped open his eyes and yelled, "Dead or alive, the stage line'll pay the reward! But I'll have died for nothin' unless Crater folks see him hung!"

The effort required to shout the words was too much for the sheriff's punished system to take. His eyes snapped close involuntarily as he slid into unconsciousness. Each breath sounded like it could be his last.

Straw stared in horror at the toe of the boot Edge had drawn back to launch in a kick at his face. Then he puffed his cheeks and emptied his

17

lungs in a cooling draught over his sweaty face when the foot was lowered gently to the ground.

"Gee, man," he rasped, needing to force his voice around his bobbing Adam's apple. "You could've broke my friggin' neck there."

"Keep that in mind, feller," Edge said evenly. "We're miles from where we're going and if you don't do what I tell you, kicking your head off your shoulders is just one way I can kill you. And I don't give a shit how the people in his hometown feel about not having a hanging to see."

"Why?" Straw demanded. "It ain't worth it, man! That bastard said it! A lousy thousand bucks!" His panicked roll away from Edge had brought him up against the carcass of the stallion. He used the hand of his good arm to get leverage on the saddle horn and push himself to his feet. His gunshot left arm hung loosely at his side. "All the way to friggin' Crater for that?"

Edge dropped his cigarette to the trail and stepped on the glowing ash. "I got nowhere else to go, feller, and it's a thousand dollars more than what's waiting for me anywhere else."

Straw shifted his intense green-eyed stare from Edge's face and moved it to and fro, shortening and lenghtening the focus, like he was seeking some visual stimulus that would trigger a line of reasoning in his racing mind to dissuade his new captor from taking him back for hanging. But nothing occurred and he abandoned the attempt. He hung his head and hunched his shoulders, his right hand reached across the front of his body to gently hold the blood-crusted bullet wound.

His tone was as dejected as his posture. "Of all

18

the lousy friggin' luck, I have to run into a money grabbin' son of a bitch like you, man."

"From where I saw it, you were running away from me, feller."

"I thought you was him!" Straw stabbed a finger toward the man with a knife in his belly. "If I'd knowed you was some cheap bounty hunter lookin' for easy pickin's—"

"Way things are, I can't be averse to being called a bounty hunter, Straw. Like to think of myself as a gambler though."

The half-breed Comanche sneered, "A chance is sure what you're takin', man. Same as me. And with a hangin' rope waitin' for me at Crater, I'm gonna be ready to risk my friggin' neck every step of the way up there. And that puts your life on the line as well."

John Hackman abruptly stopped breathing. There was no gradual slackening or any coughing or even a choking sound. His lungs simply vented what was in them and did not draw in any more.

"There goes one loser, man," Joe Straw said with a brand of evil glee. "Wonder which one of us Lady Luck plans to shit on next?"

His grinning green eyes followed Edge as the taller man moved to where John Hackman's horse stood obediently. They did not alter their expressions as the lawman's Winchester was drawn from the boot and hurled several yards from the trail.

Edge gestured with his head for the half-breed Comanche to mount the gelding.

"So okay, man. You got the top hand right now. But there can be a different deal almost anytime."

"I'm not playing your game, feller."

Straw seemed reluctant to move away from the dead horse and asked absently, "How's that, man?"

"Not making any deals," Edge answered with a cold smile that showed a sliver of teeth between his drawn lips. "Looking to hit the thousand dollar jackpot with a one armed bandit."

Chapter Three

Straw started toward Edge, but then pulled short and shook his head.

"Look, man, how'd you like to collect twice as much and no lousy trip to a one-horse town to make?"

"Like I just said. No deals."

The half-breed Comanche was having an argument with himself and his doubt showed on his weary face. Then he blurted, "Shit, I ain't gonna leave it here for some other passin' through drifter to enjoy!"

Then he swung around and backtracked to the dead horse. He was about to drop onto one knee, but froze at the sound of a gunshot and wrenched his head around as the bullet took a piece of leather out of the saddlehorn. He saw that Edge was shaking his head in a gesture of mild rebuke as he holstered the smoking Frontier Colt with less haste than he drew it.

"Ain't nothin' in the saddlebag but what's left of the money I took off the friggin' stage, man!" Straw snarled. Then he brought his emotion under control. "Best part of eighteen hundred dollars."

"Just get on the horse like you were told, feller."

Straw was on the point of accepting the challenge implicit in the other man's quietly spoken words, but then his actions jerky with anger, he moved away from the dead gray, veered to the side to snatch up his displaced derby, and jammed it on his red hair.

Edge went to the carcass and stooped to check the contents of the uppermost saddlebag. He saw that it contained a variety of well used bills.

"All right if I see if the lawman was carryin' any food, man?" Straw asked sourly. "It's a long time since I ate last."

"No sweat," Edge said as he began to take out the loosely packed money; the bills were mostly ones, fives, and tens.

He kept watch on Straw while he was doing this and saw the man bring some wax paper wrapped packages from Hackman's saddlebag. He held them in the hand, of his good arm and tore at them with his teeth to get at the food inside.

Edge ignored some coins which formed part of the stolen booty and crossed to stow the bills in one of his own saddlebags. Straw had partially appeased his ravenous hunger and was guzzling water from one of Hackman's canteens.

"Eat while you ride, feller."

Straw was totally involved with the food and drink and expressed surprise when he looked around and saw Edge astride the black mare.

"Somethin' oughta be done about my arm,

man!" he complained. "It oughta be cleaned and bandaged. Or else poison could set in."

"Maybe there's a town with a doctor in it up ahead."

"And maybe there friggin' ain't!" He spat out pieces of half-chewed food as he snarled the response. "My arm could drop off from gangrene before we find . . ."

Fear replaced anger as he backed away from the gelding and out of the path of the mare which Edge steered across the trail.

"Now what, man?" he demanded.

Edge caught hold of the gelding's bridle to turn the horse so that he headed down the slope. Then he released it, reached backwards, and landed an open-handed blow on the animal's rump. The horse snorted and lunged from a standstill into an immediate gallop. The slitted blue eyes of the mounted man looked bleakly down at Joe Straw who was staring after the dust trailing horse in aghast amazement.

"What the hell you do that for?"

"Now you have to walk until we catch up with him, feller. When your legs start to ache, it'll take your mind off that bum arm of yours. Move out, uh?"

"You're some mean bastard, man!"

Edge nodded. "And from what Hackman said, it seems I got competition."

"You don't know the friggin' half of it!" Straw snarled, tossing away a piece of wax paper as he put the stopper back in the canteen with his teeth and started to trudge in the wake of the bolting horse.

"Know my half well enough," came the evenly

voiced response as Edge set his horse moving some ten feet behind his prisoner.

The big, strong mare was as new to him as most of his clothing, purchased in Tucson some three weeks ago with a portion of reward money he had not even realized he was in line for some killing up north. There had been reason enough for them to die and so the fact that they were wanted men with a total price of fifteen hundred dollars on their heads was nothing more than a lucky break for the man called Edge.

And although he never relied upon luck, he had come to accept the bad brand philosophically and to take full advantage of the good variety. He no longer indulged in morose reflections that fortune was inclined to frown more than smile upon.

Most of his youth and early manhood had been a series of happy times shared with his parents and younger brother on a small Iowa farmstead. Only the accidental shooting of his kid brother—that made Jamie a cripple—and the peaceful passing of their parents cast shadows of regret and grief across his memories of those early years.

Next came the War Between the States and the harshest of all times. He fought as a Lieutenant and then as Captain Josiah C. Hedges of the Union cavalry. He came to accept the brutal horrors of war with something close to detached equanimity most of the time. Such an attitude kept him sane during the long, harsh years when he daily faced the danger of being killed not only by the Rebel enemy but also at the hands of six of the most vicious and amoral troopers who served the Yankee cause.

He unwittingly learned the grim lessons of sur-

24

vival that were to stand him in good stead when fate decreed he should become the man called Edge. This came in the immediate aftermath of the war's end, when he returned to find his home a burning ruin and Jamie a mutilated corpse being ravaged by buzzards.

He tracked down and killed the men who raided the Iowa farmstead, and in stepping outside the law took the new name. As Edge, he had needed to kill countless other enemies on the endless trail that had brought him to this barren valley in the Santa Rosa Mountains. Time and again, the cruel fates had conspired to lead him into situations which demanded he kill or be killed.

The fates had been implanted in him by the chain reaction of violent experiences which filled his past since the war.

Yeah, Joe Straw was right. He was a mean bastard. He had to be to stay alive while he rode the long trail from one explosion of violent trouble to the next. He never attempted anymore to avoid involvement because he had learned the hard way that there was no escape from it.

He had watched from afar as the half-breed Comanche spotted him, panicked, and made the move that proved his downfall. Then he made a move of his own, which he was prepared to admit, was a contributing factor in the death of Sheriff John Hackman.

It was a mile out along the valley floor that the black gelding had come to a halt at the end of the gallop triggered by Edge. Until they reached the quietly standing horse, the man who was walking said nothing, but occasionally directed a hate-filled glance over his shoulder at the impassively riding Edge.

The man in the saddle maintained an apparently indifferent survey in every direction, his narrowed eyes looking out from the shade of his hat brim in search of anything on the sun parched landscape that might signal danger.

There was nothing that caused him to do a double take. There was only he and his horse. The weary, resentment-burdened man was half walking and half staggering ahead of him moving toward the black gelding. A group of a half dozen buzzards gorged on the dead horse and the corpse of the young lawman behind him. Elsewhere within his range of vision, all that moved was the sun on its imperceptible crawl down the southwestern section of the cloudless sky.

"All right, man, you made your friggin' point."

Straw ran his right hand over his sweat beaded face and his green eyes met the gaze from his captor's blue eyes. Edge nodded and began to roll a cigarette while Straw hauled himself awkwardly astride the saddle of the dead Hackman's horse.

Edge lit the cigarette and said, "Point is where you ride, feller," as he flicked the dead match along the trail. "No hurry."

Straw clucked his mount forward and growled, "I couldn't if I wanted to. I'm bushed."

"What you want is of no consequence," Edge drawled as he set his own mount moving ten feet behind the man.

There was another long silence between them as Joe Straw relished the comfort of being in the saddle. This time he totally ignored the cause of

26

his predicament as he indulged his responses to pain and misery and humiliation. He began to reflect upon the stupidity of his actions that had led to his undoing. This served to sow the seeds of self anger which he soon realized was a waste of time. Time was better spent on considering the present and contemplating the future, and figuring how he could escape from the big, taciturn, cold-hearted son of a bitch who had the upper hand.

"That John Hackman was as dumb as his old man, you know that?" he said suddenly, and this time there was a slight grin on his handsome face as he glanced at his captor.

"I never knew his Pa."

Straw spat to the side as he turned to face front again. "Wasn't no valuable freight aboard the stage, man. Just a couple of rich old biddies and a couple of newlyweds with their honeymoon stake. Between them they had more money than I ever figured to make from holdin' up the stage. But it weren't near enough for that crazy old bastard to get himself killed over."

"The one ridin' guard, he did the sensible thing, man. Tossed away his gun and stuck his hands in the air. But old man Hackman, he went for a friggin' itty-bitty .38 while I had a cocked double barrel aimed at him. Can you see the sense in that?"

"No, feller."

"Right. That's right. And I can't see the sense in what you're doin', man." Another backward glance, and this time Straw expressed bewilderment with a shake of his head. "You know what I'd do if I was you and you was me?"

27

"Kill me and haul my carcass to the nearest town where the sheriff had a wanted flyer on me. Keep the stolen money and swear I'd spent it before you found me."

Another grin, which expanded to a short laugh, until the unblinking coldness in the eyes of Edge sparked renewed fear within the man. Straw swallowed hard and tried to force humor into his voice and across his face.

"Shit, man. I sure hope I ain't givin' you the idea to do that?"

"You ain't given me anything but reason to ride this trail."

Straw did a hard doubletake at Edge and decided he was telling the truth. The man would not hesitate to kill him if the circumstances were right for that, but he would not do so in cold blood.

"You got me wrong, man. I wouldn't do that at all. I'd just dump you and take off with both horses and the money from the hold-up. To hell with goin' all the way up to Crater for a lousy thousand bucks when I already got near two grand. And I wouldn't kill you. Old man Hackman and his boy? Hell, man, it was them or me. I ain't the kind that kills people without no good reason."

"Gives us some common ground, feller. So best you don't give me any reason to put you six feet under it."

"Here or in Potter's Field at Crater, man," Straw countered morosely. "What's the friggin' difference?"

"Just where you die. And how."

"You'd haul my stinkin' corpse all the way up into Colorado, man?"

"Only way I could be certain of getting the thousand dollars for you."

"You must be friggin' hard up for a buck, man!"

"Ain't that."

Straw turned in the saddle to direct scorn at Edge, "So you lied to that dumb cluck of a sheriff? You do feel bad about givin' me the chance to stick the bastard!"

"No, feller. Feel bad that he didn't get to do what he most wanted before he died."

"What the frig, man?" Straw snarled. "You never did see him nor me until today? What's it matter to you what he wanted? He's buzzard meat now! What about what I want?"

"Lost a kid brother once. Then a wife—"

"Friggin' careless of you, man!"

"Yeah it was," Edge came back evenly, accepting Straw's embittered black humor as a serious comment. "Both times I could have done something to keep them from dying—got the men who killed Jamie—way it turned out, I killed Beth myself. I ran into a lot of Indian trouble and I could have wound up dead. If I had, never was anybody around to take care of my unfinished business."

"That's crazy, you know that?"

Having snarled this, Straw remained silent and facing front for several minutes. Then he abruptly whirled in the saddle again.

"Stark ravin' friggin' crazy, man! If it was you killed your wife, all you got to do is bite on the muzzle of a gun and pull the friggin' trigger!"

"I thought about it once, feller."

29

Again the half-breed Comanche stared silently at the trail ahead in deep thought.

Then he said with less intensity, "But you ain't got the guts to do it. So you ride around the friggin' country settin' yourself up for some other guy to give you what you figure you got comin' to you?"

"You could be right."

"Could be nothin', man. Well, you just got lucky. The hangin' rope waitin' for me at the end of the line is reason enough for me to kill you. All I need now is the same kinda chance you give me to put the blade into Hackman's guts. And I'll be real happy to oblige you."

On this occasion, Joe Straw had set the Edge's mind on a train of thought. Concerning the magnetic-like force that drew him relentlessly toward the violent troubles of other people.

Fate had nothing to do with it. Instead, a deep seated guilt ordained his destiny. He was as much to blame for the way Jamie died as he was for the manner of Beth's end, and he had always known this, but he had sought to make excuses for what he did in the wake of the tragedies—claimed that he was being punished by some ethereal power over which he had no control. Yet he was motivated by the need to commit suicide by proxy, which meant the sole reason for his life was to seek death.

If that was so, why did he, after embroiling himself in each new kill or be killed situation, do his lethal best to survive at the expense of other people's lives?

"Set you to thinkin', uh man?" Joe Straw growled sneeringly. "Common ground, shit! You and me ain't no way alike. Live for the day is what I do. And never have no regrets about what I had to do to get through each one of them."

He looked back for a response, but drew none from the silent and implacable man riding behind him.

"Got you pegged, Edge. Hard as friggin' granite on the outside, but soft as marshmallow underneath. That makes you dumb, man. You're dumber even than that kid sheriff. At least he had good reason to want to bring me to Crater alive. He could see me kickin' at the end of a rope in front of all his buddies and the buddies of his old man who I killed. I can understand that. Even respect him for it. But you, you mixed-up sonofabitch, you're just usin' me to prove something to yourself."

Edge drew back his lips to show the fast-talking, half-breed Comanche a cold smile that caused a puzzled frown to spread across Straw's face.

"You through testing me, feller?"

"What man?"

"Like you said awhile back, me or the Crater hangman. You've got nothing to lose. Now you know you can't rile me into a move against you. So you'll have to figure out something different for when the time is right."

"Don't you think I friggin' won't!"

He turned to face front again with the speed of anger and his injured arm swung with momentum and erupted a groan of pain from between his gritted teeth.

"Seems you rile real easy, Joe."

The silence was different now, sullen on the part of the half-breed Comanche, easy from

Edge's point of view who, having reached the conclusion of a question at the end was content to let events provide the answer.

The afternoon ran its course and the heat shimmer lifted its sheened veil from the long valley so that in the twilight that heralded the evening, the riders could see where the trail swung eastwards to curve up the slope toward a gap between two jagged ridges.

At the point where the trail left the valley floor, Straw broke the silence. "We gonna ride all friggin' night, man?"

The sun had sunk behind the high ground to the southwest, but the sky was still lit by the glow of its setting.

"We'll find a place to bed down on the high ground, feller."

They looked harder and longer at the gap between the ridges and saw a patch of gray smoke smudging the darkening sky. Straw peered in the same direction and said, "Seems we could have company up here." He looked back at Edge and asked with a grin, "Gonna change your mind, man?"

"Keep riding. Why should I do that?"

"On account that whoever's just started that fire could be more ready to make deals than you are."

"Tell you something, Joe."

"What's that, man?"

"Easier to rile me than to scare me."

Straw did not look around again, but kept his attention fixed upon the pass as night closed in over the mountains so that the smoke could no longer be seen. The fire, if it was out in the open, was not large enough to give off a glow that could be seen from this distance.

"It's all right for you," the half-breed Comanche said at length, the apprehensiveness—visible in his rigid posture astride the saddle—sounding in his tense voice. "You're armed and behind me. They could be dry gulchers up there. The kind that shoot first and then find out what kinda people it is they've shot."

"For a feller that claims to live for the day, you sure are a worrier, Joe," Edge drawled.

"I got friggin' cause, ain't I? Ridin' with a crazy man who's got a death wish. And me with nothin' to protect myself with."

Still he concentrated his anxious attention on the gap in the high ground which was starting to be illuminated by the light of the rising new moon. Now he kept his voice to a hoarse whisper, as if afraid his protest would last more than half a mile to the pass.

"You're wrong, feller."

"Keep your damn voice down," Straw snarled softly.

"You got me to protect you," Edge said at the same level as before.

The half-breed Comanche whirled in the saddle again, his face contorted by a scowl that was part fear, rage, and derision.

"Shit, man!" he rasped.

"I ain't got the need, feller. But unless you want them to smell us before they hear us, best you keep a tight ass."

Chapter Four

Straw remained in a state of tension until he and Edge rode to the summit of the grade and reined their horses. They were able to look along the trail that ran northwards on a slight downslope with a sheer rock escarpment rising to fifty feet on the left and an equally steep drop of twice this much to the right. This ledge was two trail widths wide and ran for perhaps a quarter-mile before it broadened into an expansive hillside littered with countless chunks of rocks, falling away to reach to the narrow stream that hugged the base of the lower cliff and fed a pool at the lowest point of the rocky hill.

The fire was built in an arc of rocks where the ledge broadened onto the hill and in its glow Edge and Joe Straw could see two men and a mule.

The animal had been relieved of its burden of packs and was hobbled. One of the men was pouring two cups of coffee and the other was stirring a cooking pot over the fire when the riders at the pass first saw them. Both were short of stature, with beards and stooped shoulders, and the slowness of their movements further suggested that they were old timers.

"Prospectors, looks like," Straw said, still whispering. "Their kind can be real unfriendly sons of bitches."

Edge made a one-handed bullhorn around his mouth and yelled, "Hey, you fellers welcome strangers?"

Both men were drinking coffee, and they hurled their cups down and dropped their hands to drape holstered revolvers as they wrenched their heads around to peer up at the pass.

Joe Straw vented a cry of alarm at Edge's shout and the men's response, then made to jerk at his reins and turn his mount. Edge had drawn up alongside his prisoner to the left, and he swung his right arm up and across, the fingers of the hand stretched straight and stiff in order to land a sharp, edge-of-the-hand blow against the poisoned and blood-crusted area of Straw's swollen upper arm.

The half-breed Comanche's shrill scream of agony was amplified by the echo effect between the rock faces flanking the pass. There was a wet sound of vomit as the fear and pain erupted an evil smelling stream of half-digested food from the man's stomach and spewed it from his gaping mouth. He pitched sideways off the horse and was unconscious before he crashed to the ground and rolled over onto his side by which time the hand that delivered the blow had streaked forward to grip the reins released by Straw. The turn of the gelding was halted.

"What the hell is going on up there?" one of the

men among the rocks roared, his voice broad with a Scottish accent.

"Nothing for you fellers to worry about!" Edge called. "Long as you don't draw those handguns against me!"

"Talk sense, Yank!" the other prospector countered, his accent revealing the same Scottish nationality.

Both voices confirmed the initial impression that the men bathed in fireglow and moonlight were not young.

"Listen and it has to make sense to you! You can aim those revolvers at me, but you won't have any chance of dropping me at this range! And anyone aims a gun at me after I've told him not to, I kill him!"

While Edge's shouted words were still resounding between the cliff faces to either side, the two men exchanged brief words of their own, not loud enough to carry up the trail to the pass.

"What it is you want of us, stranger?"

"A share of your fire is all! Or if we ain't welcome, no trouble!"

"What'd you do to the man with you, stranger?"

"You fellers scared him! I calmed him down!"

There was another brief, low-voiced exchange between the prospectors while Straw breathed regularly and Edge waited patiently.

"All right, Yank! You can visit with us and be welcome! Angus and I have no desire for trouble! But we are not without experience of dealing with it if it comes unbidden!"

"Obliged!" Edge responded, and swung out of his saddle. Then he hefted the limp form of Joe

Straw up from the ground and draped him face down over the saddle of the gelding, taking hold of the reins of both horses in his left hand as he started to lead them along the trail's ledge.

His right hand swung slightly at his side, nevermore than a few inches from the butt of the Frontier Colt jutting from his holster.

Neither Scotsman was touching his revolver now, but both were obviously tense and ready to draw should the approaching stranger do so.

The hooves of the horses thudded on the trail, the fire crackled, and at the foot of the sheer drop, the stream made muted trickling noises.

The tension increased as each man realized the gap was reduced to effective revolver range.

Edge saw that Angus and his partner were over sixty years of age. Angus was a head shorter at about five feet, slightly built but with a suggestion of wiry strength in his frame which was clothed in a ragged checked shirt, a suit jacket, and unmatched pants tucked into knee high boots. On his head was an ancient army forage cap with the insignia missing.

The taller Scot was powerfully built and the muscles of his chest bulged the undershirt, which was all he wore beneath a sheepskin coat. The cuffs of his pants were worn outside his boots. His hat was of the Texas style.

The men's flesh was as filthy as their clothing and the gray beards that left only their upper cheeks, eyes, and brows exposed were matted and unkempt.

They smelled bad, but no worse than the half-breed Comanche.

Edge raised his right hand away from the holstered gun and touched the brim of his hat. "Evening to you," he greeted evenly.

"And you, Yank. This is Angus Stewart and I am called Robert McBride."

"Edge. The one sleeping is Joe Straw."

He had led the two horses into the circle of firelight within the arc of rocks. Now he halted and released the reins, turned to lift the unconscious man down from the saddle.

"It's an Indian, Robert!" Stewart exclaimed with unpleasant surprise.

"Half breed," Edge corrected as he lowered Straw gently to the ground on his back.

"We offer no hospitality to any variety of Indian," McBride said grimly.

Edge straightened up. "He killed the driver of a stage. I'm taking him back to where it happened so he can be hanged."

McBride shot a questioning glance at Stewart and received a shrug.

"In that case, Mr. Edge, we will make an exception. We have coffee to share. It would be better for us if you have your own food to add to the cooking pot."

"No sweat."

Edge led the horses over to where the mule was hobbled and removed their saddles. He hobbled them and carried both sets of gear back to the side of the fire. Where the two Scots were seated on the mule packs, drinking coffee and dividing their curious attention between Edge and Straw.

"What's in the pot?"

"Beans and black-eyed peas," Stewart answered.

Edge dropped the gear and unfastened one of

his own saddlebags. "Let's live it up a little," he said and tossed some cubes of dried meat into the steaming pot of vegetables.

Then, watched with increasing curiosity by the prospectors, he took out his own cooking pot, filled it with water from a canteen and set it on the fire.

"You will not drink our coffee?" McBride asked sourly.

"Be a pleasure," Edge told him, and filled his own cup from the pot on the fringe of the fire. Edge sat on the hard ground and leaned against the pile of gear, took a sip of the strong, black coffee before explaining with a wave of his free hand, "He's got a bullet hole in his arm. Past time when it should have been cleaned up."

McBride nodded after a longer look at the prostrate Straw. "That explains how you felled him with a single blow up there."

"You are a lawman, Mr. Edge?" Stewart asked.

"No, feller."

"But you said you were taking him back there to face the gallows?"

"As a favor to a lawman he killed."

"There is a bounty on him," McBride guessed.

"That, too."

"A large bounty?" Stewart asked quickly, and received a glowering glance from his partner.

Edge showed a cold grin that caused his eyes and teeth to glitter in the firelight. "No gold in these here hills?"

Stewart hastened to place a different interpretation on his query. "Do not misunderstand me, laddie. I have good cause to hate Indians. When Robert and I came here from Edinburgh my wife was with us. In the Dakotas Black Hills our claim was raided by Indians. A year ago almost to the day. Elizabeth was no longer young. But that did not prevent the savages from taking her by turns. It was of shame that she died, not a week later."

"We were away from the claim, hunting food, when it happened," McBride added quickly as he saw the cold grin leave Edge's features, displaced by a tight-lipped, narrow-eyed expression of deeply felt bitterness.

"They were full-blooded Sioux in that part of the country," he rasped. "I told you fellers Straw's a half breed. Indian half Comanche or maybe Apache."

"Comanche, on my Ma's side," Joe Straw supplied weakly and turned his head to look with pain-filled eyes at the startled prospectors. "And take it easy. Edge here ain't mad at you. He ain't got a wife no more on account of Indian trouble. Were they Sioux, man?"

He had lifted his head off the ground and was gazing at Edge when he posed the question.

Straw's guess was right. His abrupt change of mood was caused by Stewart's story triggering vivid memories of his wife's death. And because the Scotsman's tale parallelled that long ago time of fear, anger, and grief in so many details, Edge was affected by it to a far greater degree than on any other occasion he could recall.

It had been the Sioux who hit the neat little farmstead in the Dakotas. And his wife's name was Elizabeth.

On his own time scale, he seemed to be locked inside a private world of harsh memories for many minutes while his mind was attacked by disjointed, out-of-sequence images of how his best of all possible worlds had been shattered by the Sioux uprising. But when he had won the struggle to drive the painful past back where it belonged and was again aware of the trio of men staring at him, none of their expressions suggested more than a couple of seconds had gone by.

"Lost more than a wife in my time," he told the bearded prospectors evenly. "A lot of it to white men. Don't blame every stranger I come across for what others did."

"You're entitled to your opinion, laddie, Stewart allowed grimly, and now looked at Straw who was stretched out flat on his back again, lacking the strength even to keep his head up from the ground. "But I have never trusted an Indian from that day to this. And you told Robert and me yourself that this one has killed two men."

"Aye, you did, Yank," McBride confirmed.

"And he'll hang for it, like I said."

Stewart nodded. "That prospect is pleasing to me, laddie. My question about the size of the bounty was to seek assurance that you have sufficient cause to complete the journey to the gallows."

"For if you did not, Angus would be pleased to rid the world of the savage," McBride added.

Straw forced his head up off the ground again to direct a pleading look at Edge after glaring at the two quiet spoken Scotsmen.

"You said you'd protect me, Edge! They still got irons in their holsters! And they hate me just 'cause there's some Indian in me! I think we should get the hell away from ..."

He was trying to rise, but the fresh pain erupted by the blow to his injured arm intensified with every move. And he flopped back down again with a groan that spilled saliva from between his quivering lips.

"Aim to see he hangs, feller," Edge told Stewart as he set down his empty coffee cup and lifted the pot of boiling water off the fire. "Even if I have to kill anyone who has different ideas."

He rose and went to Straw's side. The punished man looked at the pot he was carrying and scowled, "My gut's still churnin'. I try to get anythin' inside me, it'll come right up again."

"Hot water is all."

Edge lowered the pot to the ground and returned to bring the dead Hackman's bedroll. The two prospectors watched him stoically as he unfurled the blankets and rerolled one to make a pillow which he eased under Straw's head. Then their interest heightened and the injured halfbreed felt fear more strongly than pain as Edge reached into the long hair at the nape of his neck and drew the straight razor from the concealed pouch.

"You ain't gonna cut me, man?"

"Like you told these fellers, take it easy, Joe."

"I'd rather take my chance of gangrene settin' in!"

His voice was shrill, but then he sucked in a great gulp of air and exhaled it as a sigh. Edge used the razor to cut two strips from the blank, one of them narrow, which he left whole. The other was broader and he cut this into squares.

"Going to try to clean out whatever dirt got into the wound, Joe. Then bind it up to keep it clean."

43

"Gee, man. That's gonna hurt like hell, ain't it?"

"No worse than your knife in Hackman's belly."

The bearded Scots had finished their coffee and now Stewart refilled both cups.

"Something I've never understood, Robert."

"What is that, Angus?"

"Why it is that adult male Indians are called braves."

"It is strange indeed, Angus. Perhaps that is why their skin is red. The better to hide the yellow that's inside."

Straw brought his head up off the blanket pillow to glower at the men and snarl, "Shut your stinkin' mouths! I'd like to see you sons of bitches go through what I been through and wind up friggin' laughin'! And I'd like it even better if I was the one that put bullets into you and then beat up on where—"

Once more his high pitched scream cut through the mountain air, sounding to the men close to him that it had the power and volume to reach through the night into infinity. The keening cry forced from his stretched throat by Edge's action of pressing the boiled water soaked wad of blanket against the pus closed entry hole of the rifle bullet.

Joe Straw, intent upon bawling out Stewart and McBride, was totally unprepared for the excruciating agony exploded by the scalding water against his poisoned flesh. And his physical and vocal reaction to it were short lived. This new punishment was too much for his system to accept. The scream was curtailed, the rigidity drained from his body, and he was again plunged into unconsciousness, his head slamming hard back down onto the pillow.

Both Scotsmen winced, as if they had vicariously experienced a degree of pain themselves.

Edge removed the compress and began to bathe away the thick, evil smelling pus that had burst from the mouth of the wound.

"You think he will be grateful that you put him out before doing that, laddie?"

"I don't care what he thinks, feller. Happens to be easier for me to do this while he ain't yelling and thrashing about."

They sipped their coffee and remained silent while Edge completed his primitive treatment of the oblivious man, cleaning both the entry and exit wound and then binding the arm.

The fire crackled and the pot bubbled, keeping the coldness of the night at bay and permeating the atmosphere of the camp with the appetizing aroma of woodsmoke and cooking food.

Then, as Edge washed his hands in the cooled water and dried them on the remains of the cut blanket, McBride said, "He would have been less trouble to you had you not done that, Yank."

"And since he is condemned to die in any event, laddie?" Stewart added with arched eyebrows.

"Supper smells like it's ready to eat," Edge said, moving back to their side of the fire, but this time he sat on the saddles and delved into the center of his bedroll to bring out his plate and spoon.

There was a ladle in the pot and he transferred a heap of stew on to his plate and began to eat.

McBride shrugged his shoulders and his partner grunted, each in his own way expressing resignation to the close mouthed nature of their visitor. They helped themselves from the pot and for several minutes all three ate the food with scant show of relish. The beards of the prospectors became more matted with greasy gravy and morsels of meat and vegetables which dropped unheeded from the fast moving spoons.

They finished first and lit ready-filled pipes. They waited until Edge was through eating and had lit a freshly rolled cigarette.

"The savage, laddie? Did he get much of a haul off the stage he robbed?"

Edge slid down off the saddles and leaned his shoulders against them. "The money doesn't matter. He killed the driver. Dead man's son was the sheriff who came after him."

"And the Indian killed him, too?"

"That's what happened, McBride. After the sheriff put that bullet hole in Straw's arm."

"And you just happened to be passing?" Stewart asked.

Edge pursed his lips. "You fellers want to come right out and say it? Or is beating about the bush some old Scots custom you aim to spread around this country?"

"We are simply passing the time of day," Stewart muttered peevishly.

"If you find our company distasteful, it is not our wish that you should stay here," his partner added.

"Out in the hills we see few strangers, laddie and have exhausted conversation between ourselves."

"Never hit any paydirt worth talking about, uh?"

"You have a suspicious mind, Yank!" McBride snarled, scowling through the smoke curling up from the bowl of his pipe. "That is the second time you have spoken of our obvious impoverishment."

"Suspicious mind is right, Robert!" Stewart agreed sourly. "The man has completely misunderstood me again."

"Americans!" McBride growled, and spat into the fire. "They all want to be rich and are prepared to go to any lengths to get their desire. They think everyone else has the same ambition. And the same lack of scruples."

"It is simply that I am a student of my fellow man, laddie," Stewart said with less rancor. He directed a look of reprimand at his partner. "And I have no quarrel with the particular aspect of the American dream Robert takes issue with."

He looked again at McBride, who snorted and got wearily to his feet to gather up the dirty dishes.

"And he has no right to speak as he does. After all, did we both not abandon safe and humdrum lives as clerks in Edinburgh, and sell all we possessed, against the advice of our friends, to travel to your country in the hope of finding our pot of gold? And have I not lost my dear wife in the pursuit of—"

"It is an honest line of work we are in, Angus," McBride grumbled, as he used the dry, gritty dirt on the fringe of the camp to get the congealed food off the plates.

"Aye, Robert. But who are we—relative strangers in this new land—to take exception to the trade of this laddie? Edinburgh has it's crimi-

47

nal element sure enough, and a well trained body of the constabulary to deal with it. Out here in this vast land, an incalculable number of constables would be required to ensure that those guilty of crime get their just deserts."

He surveyed Edge quizzically. Edge tossed the butt of his cigarette into the dying fire and shifted into an apparently more comfortable position against the heap of gear. He tipped his hat forward slightly, but not so much that the brim obscured his view of Angus Stewart some four feet from him and Robert McBride who was now urinating between two of the rocks on the fringe of the firelight.

"International understanding ain't a subject that interests me, feller," he murmured sleepily as he began to scratch the left side of his neck.

"I have wandered away from my point, laddie. I am intrigued by the value placed upon human life in this part of the world, the amount of money that Indian obtained for killing the driver of the stagecoach. And you intrigue me, laddie. Without wishing to insult you, you do not strike me as the kind of man to—"

"Now, Angus!" McBride roared.

He had rebuttoned the front of his pants and turned sideways on to the fire, so that his right hip on which the holstered Colt hung was out of sight of Edge's seemingly unwatchful eyes. But his bent elbow showed at his back when his right hand moved from the front of his pants to fist around the butt of the revolver.

An instant before he voiced the warning to his partner and drew the Colt as he whirled to face his target. He was given a clear shot by Stewart hurling himself sideways off the pack to sprawl on the ground.

They had a smooth working partnership which would have succeeded if Edge had been as genuinely at ease as he appeared. They had showed just the right degree of distrust for the night visitors to their camp. Their inquisitiveness was justified by the captor-captive relationship of the intruders. They had carefully tested Edge's to both friendly and reproachful overtures and settled for the age old combination of nice feller allied with bastard.

But they had unwittingly foreseen the flaw in their murderous plan when they agreed Edge had a suspicious mind. He had been ready to counter whatever aggressive move they made since he first joined them at their camp fire. Behind his outward appearance or contented weariness, he became increasingly tensed to react with every broadly Scottish accented word that Angus Stewart spoke while his partner attended to the dishes. His distrust of the two prospectors heightened because McBride made no attempt to get behind him.

As McBride began the turn and yelled the warning, his hooded, almost closed eyes saw that Stewart was no immediate threat. He dropped his left hand away from the position where it was a fraction of a second away from drawing the razor, pressed the palm to the ground to add power to his counter move, and at the same time his right came up from the ground, fingers hooked to bring the Colt from his holster. The thumb cocked the hammer and the forefinger curled to the trigger.

The flickering firelight illuminated the fear in

Robert McBride's eyes and in that instant the Scot with the gun in his hand realized he and Stewart had made a fatal misjudgment. He was not fast enough, because the expected element of surprise had never existed.

The Frontier Colt in Edge's hand exploded a shot before McBride's raking revolver was within a foot of coming on target. The bullet hit him on a rising trajectory that started almost at ground level, blasted into his chest left of center and was deflected into a more acute elevation when it glanced off a bone of the ribcage, bored a hole through the upper area of his heart, and cracked a shoulder blade as it came to rest.

The impact of the bullet added momentum to his turn and he almost completed a flat-footed pirouette before death drained his body of rigidity, and he collapsed into a heap, covering the drying stain where he had urinated and now spurting blood onto the thirsty ground.

Edge had powered up into a half crouch the instant the killing shot left his Colt. Before McBride was a falling corpse lunging forward. He crashed down heavily on the prone form of Angus Stewart who was fumbling desperately to get his own revolver clear of the holster as he tried to roll over onto his back.

Two hundred pounds of falling weight thudded him face down again and rushed air from his lungs with an explosive sound. The man had no breath in his body to utter a vocal response to the pain of being crushed nor to the more intense agony when Edge pressed the muzzle of the Frontier Colt against the elbow of Stewart's right arm and triggered a second shot. The man's hand gave up the struggle to draw his gun.

Edge thumbed back the hammer and shifted his weight as he rose onto his knees and then his haunches. He aimed the gun at the side of Stewart's head from a range of three inches as the winded and wounded man stayed flat on the ground, struggling for breath and grimacing at his pain.

"Cost of living depends on a man's tastes, feller," Edge rasped through gritted teeth. "Dying for your partner was the price of one shell. For you, I'll double it."

Stewart had one side of his face pressed hard to the ground so that Edge could see only his left eye. It expressed the sadness of disappointment, at odds with the grimace of pain that contorted the rest of his bearded face.

"Why be so generous, laddie?" he asked with difficulty.

"Got a question I'd like answered."

"Robert and I have never given up looking for the lucky strike, laddie. But it was not to be. There were five men before you, lacking your guile, but we had the same misfortune as in our pursuit of gold from the ground. We never obtained more than enough to feed ourselves and the animal."

He was still suffering chronic breathing difficulty, needing to fight to get out each word.

"Ain't your hard luck that interests me, feller. Need to know if you really did have a wife called Elizabeth who was killed by the Sioux up in the Dakotas."

Despite his suffering, Angus Stewart was briefly

intrigued by the query. "Quite a coincidence, if what the Indian said was true. Aye, laddie. It happened as I said it did. And if that gentle woman had not perished after the savages attacked her . . . Robert and I would not have done the evil that we did. Elizabeth was his sister, you understand."

"Obliged," Edge said absently.

"You, too? If your woman had not. . . ?"

"Never will know."

"You'll finish me now, I'm thinking?"

"No doubt about that."

Stewart closed his eye Edge could see and murmured, "I have no complaint, laddie."

Edge squeezed the trigger and his impassive expression did not alter as the neat hole appeared in Stewart's temple and the man's nervous system caused an involuntary spasm to jerk him briefly from head to toe. A few droplets of blood sprayed away from the wound and fell into his matted beard.

"Got to agree with you, feller," he growled as he came erect and slid the Colt back into his holster. "Ain't no more natural cause to die from than trying to kill me."

Then he crossed to where McBride was crumpled, took hold of the collar of his coat and dragged him from among the rocks. He took hold of the corpse of Stewart in his free hand and dragged both away from the camp fire out onto the ledge along which the stage coach trail ran. He arranged them side by side on the rim of the precipice. Then, with a booted foot, he tipped them over the cliff.

The limp and unfeeling bodies seemed held together for a few feet, then separated and the heavier McBride tumbled ahead of his partner. McBride smashed to the rocky bank of the stream perhaps a full second before Stewart's flesh was burst and his bones shattered some six feet closer to the trickling water. In the glittering moonlight the unmoving forms were dark silhouettes against the gray rocks.

"Man, did I have you figured wrong," Joe Straw gasped as Edge returned to the area of light and warmth radiated by the fire.

"Welcome back to the land of the living, feller," Edge answered evenly.

"I been here since you blasted the first of them sons of bitches, man. It ain't no death wish you got. You just gotta kill people, ain't you?"

Edge made no reply to the half-breed Comanche who continued to lay on his back, still able only to turn his head on the blanket pillow. He did not even look at the wan-faced, injured man as he hauled the mule packs away from the camp to tip them one at a time over the cliff top.

"You're a friggin' mad man!" Straw accused, wide eyes fixed upon his captor as Edge came back to the half circle of rocks again and released the mule from his hobbles. He made no move to drive the animal from the camp. "There could have been somethin' worth havin' in them packs."

"I got everything I need, feller," Edge told him, and squatted down at Straw's feet. He used the rope which had hobbled the mule to tie the man's ankles together.

"I ain't never seen a more cold-blooded killin'! And for friggin' nothin'!"

"For the same reason as McBride, feller.

53

Warned both of them not to aim a gun at me. Both of them tried it."

"Wasn't shootin' them enough for you, man? Why'd you have to toss their bodies over the friggin' cliff?"

"Didn't smell too sweet when they were alive. Down there, their rotting carcasses won't bother me."

After binding Straw's ankles together, there was enough spare rope to thread through the handles of the Scotmens' tin cups and tie them so that they would rattle at any slight movement the man made.

"Shit, I thought I was a friggin' hard case, man," the half-breed Comanche rasped. "But I ain't even through the first grade of the school you're at."

Edge had left him to toss a pile of brush onto the dying fire that the ill-fated prospectors had gathered after taking the cooking and coffee pots off the embers.

"You want anything to eat, Joe?" he asked.

Straw made a face. "I'd throw it right up again, man. Not on account of my arm hurtin' like hell. Just thinkin' about you makes my damn stomach churn."

"Your decision," Edge said flatly, and dragged the two saddles and his bedroll further away from the flames which were fiercely consuming the fresh fuel. He broadened the gap between himself and Straw. He unfurled his blankets and got between them with the Winchester for company, resting his head on a saddle and tilting his hat far enough forward to cover his eyes.

"You ain't a man to take no chances, are you?"

Straw growled when the roar of the flames had subsided.

"School's out, feller. Sleeping time."

"How am I supposed to get to sleep, man! With my arm feelin' like it's burnin' hotter than the friggin' fire?"

Edge raised a hand to lift his hatbrim so that he could meet the angry gaze of Straw.

"I ain't no doctor, feller," he said coldly. "But I'm willing to give you the same kind of treatment that put you out twice before."

The half-breed Comanche scowled. "Thanks but no thanks, man. I'd rather suffer."

The hat brim dropped back to cover most of Edge's face. "Obliged if you'd do it in silence."

"Tell you what'd help, man."

"I don't know any lullabies."

"If you had some liquor, I could keep that down and it would maybe help with the pain."

"Never carry it, Joe."

"There might've been some in them packs you tossed away, damnit!"

Beneath the brim of the Stetson, Edge's mouth-line formed into the semblance of a sardonic smile. "Obliged, feller," he murmured. "You've given me a beautiful thought to sleep on."

"What's that, crazy man?"

The tip of Edge's tongue emerged to run between his lips. "Couple of Scotch on the rocks. Water on the side."

Chapter Five

The rattle of the tin cups brought Edge to instant awareness only once during the night. With one hand fisting tigher around the frame of the Winchester, he raised his hat with the other to peer across at Joe Straw. The half-breed Comanche was in a deep sleep of mental and physical exhaustion and it was just an involuntary movement of his legs that caused the noise.

The half-breed Mexican drifted easily back to sleep, untroubled by doubts about what had happened in the past or worries concerned with the future. He was not disturbed again until the cold dawn had broken and the first shaft of warm sunlight lanced in from the east.

When he rose, he stirred the gray ashes to find some glowing embers and tossed brush on them to set the fire going again. He filled his own and the dead men's coffee pots, but put grounds in only one of them. He washed up, shaved, and drank two cups of coffee before Joe Straw groaned into the waking world and cried out from the sharp pain when he moved his wounded arm in an attempt to flex the numbness out of it.

It took perhaps five seconds for his green eyes to focus on the brightly sunlit scene and for his mind to be triggered into recalling the events which led to being here.

"Morning, Joe."

Edge filled John Hackman's cup and reached out to hand it to Straw, who accepted it with a scowl after he had eased himself gingerly into a sitting posture.

Then, he growled grudgingly, "Thanks," after taking several sips of the coffee.

"No sweat. You figure you can face breakfast without throwing up?"

"All I've ate in two friggin' days was that stuff you allowed me outta Hackman's saddlebags, man. I gotta have somethin' decent inside me to get through this one."

Edge nodded and tossed some dried ingredients from his supplies into his cooking pot and set it on the fire.

"I gotta keep this hobble on my legs, man?"

"Until we're ready to leave, feller."

"No friggin' chances at all!"

"Appears you left it a little late in learning your lessons."

Edge sprinkled some chili powder in the pot and began to stir the food while Straw seemed to give all his embittered attention to the coffee he was drinking. The sun rose over the ragged horizon to the east and the last of the night's chill was driven from the air in this part of the mountains.

"I suppose I oughta thank you, man," the half-breed Comanche said at length.

"You already did for the coffee. And half the breakfast is for me."

"I mean for handlin' them two murderin' sons of bitches last night. If they'd blasted you to hell, I wouldn't've been far behind, I figure."

"It wasn't any trouble, Joe."

"I friggin' saw that, man. But I had no call to sound off at you the way I did. They deserved what you give them and no mistake."

Edge rolled, lit, and smoked his first cigarette of the day while Straw took regular sips of his coffee. The sun's warmth increased, the fire crackled, and the food bubbled. The cooking chili began to smell good.

"I gotta thank you for takin' care of my arm, as well," the half-breed Comanche said at length. "I sure wasn't ready to do that when you started in with the hot water. But if you hadn't cleaned up where I was hit, it'd feel a whole lot worse this mornin', I figure."

He set down his empty cup and gently massaged the blanket binding covering the wound.

Edge ladled out breakfast on his and John Hackman's plate and gave one to his prisoner.

"Thanks, man."

Edge tossed the cigarette butt on the fire and growled with a grimace, "You planning to make me throw up, feller?"

"What?"

"You hate my guts, so you figure to give me a pain with all this gratitude you're spreading around?"

"Shit, man! I mean it! Shape I'm in I gotta rely on you for every friggin' thing! Just want you to know you could've done a whole lot worse at it so far."

Straw's sour response seemed to be born out of

genuine pique at Edge's coldly skeptical reception of his attempt to express gratitude. There was even a strong suggestion of hurt in his green eyes.

"I'm taking you up to Colorado to be hanged for murder, feller. You got nothing to thank me for."

"You don't think so, man? I'm the bastard son of a Comanche squaw who was raped by a drunk Irishman! That don't make for no easy life, I can tell you! But life's mighty friggin' sweet, whatever kind you got! There's a whole lot of miles between here and Crater, man! And a whole lot of things can happen from here to there! So I sure as hell am grateful not to be dead from you gettin' taken in by those two sons of bitches you tossed over the cliff! And I'm happy I ain't gonna die of gangrene!"

"Eat your breakfast, feller."

Straw allowed the anger to drain out of him, and then showed a bright grin. "And that's another thing, man. With you around, I ain't gonna starve to death."

"While you wait for a chance to bite the hand that feeds you, uh?"

The grin was held on the dark skinned, good looking face that—for the first time—Edge realized did not sprout bristles. "You wouldn't expect me to promise you nothin', man? My old lady—the squaw I told you about—one time down in Sonora, I needed some fast money to pay off a guy who was gonna kill me. I sold her to a bunch of real mean Mexicans. A man who'll sell his mother into slavery, man? You wouldn't expect him to tell you he ain't gonna kill you first chance he gets—to keep from being hung?"

Edge continued to eat, showing not a flicker of emotion in reaction to Straw's revelation, finished his breakfast, and took the other man's still heaped plate from him.

"Hey, I ain't—"

"Big talker, small eater, feller. We're going to leave now."

He scraped the remains of the food onto the fire and cleaned the utensils. Then he furled the bedrolls, packed away the gear, and saddled the mare and the gelding.

"Man, you're so mean, I'm surprised you don't poison yourself when you swallow your spit!" Straw snarled.

Now Edge grinned as he dropped to his haunches and untied the man's ankles, tossing the tin cups away.

"That's better, Joe," he drawled. "Best we keep on the way we started. Then there won't be any hard feelings when I hand you over to the people at Crater."

He held out a hand to help Straw to his feet, but the injured man sneered at the offer and tried to rise unaided. He couldn't make it and with hatred spread over his sweat beaded face he was forced to accept assistance.

"I gotta take a leak, man."

"Fire needs dousing, feller."

Edge waited near the horses and the mule while Straw struggled with one hand to unbutton and then refasten the front of his pants, his left arm hanging limply at his side. When the half-breed Comanche was done, he used a foot to scrape dirt onto the embers that continued to glow.

He did not try to shun Edge's help in getting

astride the gelding. Then his captor mounted the mare and they set off down the sloping trail. The mule followed them.

At the base of the hill, where the stream emptied into the pool, Edge called a halt. Straw eyed him with resentful expectation.

"What now?"

"Bath time, feller."

"You're kiddin' man?" he said with a grin of anticipated pleasure.

Edge swung out of his saddle. "We both stink, feller. Least we can get rid of what ails us on the outside."

He started to take off his clothes and Straw was able to dismount without help and follow the other man's example.

The two horses and the mule drank eagerly from the side of the pool, then cropped at the grass that fringed it.

With less to take off, Straw was the first to strip naked and wade out into the water far enough away from the bank so that he was able to sit down with his head just above the surface.

Edge still had the beaded thong with the razor pouch encircling his neck when he entered the pool which had already been warmed by the sun. He did not go in so deeply as Straw, lowered himself with relish into the water at a point between the half-breed Comanche and the bank.

The prisoner's beam of pure enjoyment revealed that the man's thoughts were far removed from any idea of trying to get to the Colt in the discarded gunbelt or the Winchester jutting from the boot on the feeding mare.

"That bastard Hackman didn't even let me

wash up, let alone take a friggin' bath," Straw said after ducking his head under the surface and beginning to scrub with his good hand in his red curly hair. "Kept my hands tied the whole damn time and spoonfed me when he felt like it. Said I was a dangerous wild animal and he was gonna treat me like one. Four friggin' days he had me. Ridin' twenty four hours and sleepin' four. And with the son of a bitch so close behind me when I got away from him, I didn't have no chance to let up. And nothin' to eat, either."

Edge doused himself all over then stood up to rub at ingrained dirt in his skin with a kerchief.

"Man, this is real luxury."

Edge did not relax his survey of the apparently deserted mountainscape that surrounded them while he took the bath.

"You know, I'm pretty evenly divided between that Irish rapist and the squaw he took, Edge. And I don't mean just in the way I look. She was okay. Come to hate the Comanches for makin' her an outcast just because she allowed herself to get raped by a white. Allowed herself, shit. But she had self-respect, you know what I mean? Like in keepin' herself clean best she was able. Stuff like that. All Indians do that, you know. Take care of things like that a whole lot better than a whole lot of whites.

"The rapist, he was a real no-good son of a bitch, way the squaw told me. And I gotta believe I went bad on account of his blood that's in my veins. Got to know the squaw pretty good and never knowed her to do harm to any livin' thing. Just spoke a lot of evil about the Comanches that kicked her out through no fault of her own."

63

He ducked under the water again and when he surfaced, Edge was out of the pool and starting to towel himself dry with his shirt.

"And me being half-and-half the way I am, I can see her point of view. Double, man. I'm on the outside of the Indians and the whites both."

Now he rose and began to wade out of the pool. He asked, "You listenin' to what I'm saying, Edge?"

"Sure, Joe. And you ain't like that old prospector last night. Fishing to find out if I had the money you took off the stage. You've got plenty of time to get to the point."

Straw nodded and began to dress without drying the beads of water from his muscular flesh. "I sure ain't fishin' for sympathy, man. If anyone needs it, I figure you do. But you ain't the kind open to it and I sure ain't the kind to give it. So I ain't gettin' to no point you care about. Guess what I'm sayin' is that, apart from havin' a hangin' rope waitin' for me at the end of the line, I'd rather be me than you. Whatever I am."

Edge buttoned his shirt and tucked it into the waistband of his pants.

"Least I make the best outta friggin' life, man. The ups and the downs. Why, you're so stone faced I can't see you ever havin' any fun. Don't you ever friggin' unbend and have a good belly laugh at anythin'? No, course you don't! You're hardly human, you know that?"

"Death ain't a laughing matter, feller. You want a hand up onto your horse?"

"I can do it now, man. You've had a whole night's sleep since you killed them two."

At the third cursing attempt he managed to

haul himself astride the gelding. Then he looked with a scornful grin at Edge who was carrying his canteens toward the mare after filling them from the stream above the pool.

"It's your death I'm talking about, Joe."

"Mine or yours, man."

Edge hung the canteens from the saddle horn and climbed astride his mount. Nodded and answered: "Yeah, I figure it'll be a matter of who laughs last laughing longest."

Straw spat into the pool. "Be my pleasure to put you outta your misery."

Edge heeled his horse forward and gestured for the half-breed Comanche to restart the trip. "And if it turns out to be the other way around, feller, I'll do my laughing. All the way to the bank."

Chapter Six

Edge had known from the time he first started to follow the trail—a few hours before he saw Joe Straw riding it—that it still had some purpose. Its surface showed little sign of use, yet it was not disused.

Like so many other trails that crisscrossed the southwestern territories, it had probably been originated by the Indians as they moved in great numbers to the dictates of the passing seasons. Then a few migrant whites, seeking a hospitable piece of terrain on which to settle, had further compacted the dirt. Next the army, in greater numbers and with more heavily laden wagons had made use of the route that offered the easiest way to journey through the mountains from north to south or vice versa.

There were just a handful of army posts in the area now, a token military presence to protect the few settlers who had staked claims to scattered pieces of poor land against the small number of Indians who survived the brutal occupation and refused to retreat to less hospitable regions of the territories.

There were relatively recent wheeltracks and hoofprints on the trail. Edge guessed these marked the to and fro passages of a stage coach between widely-spaced communities or maybe the wagons of a freight line company. Whichever, there had to be way stations of some sort to cater for the needs of trail-weary horses, drivers, and passengers.

At mid-morning, he and Joe Straw caught their first glimpse of such a place in the far distance, a single-story building with smoke rising from a chimney on the outside of an end wall. The view was blurred by heat shimmer for several minutes, then came into sharp focus as they rode closer. They could see to the right of the trail from their viewpoint, at a point where their way ran out of the northern ridges of the Santa Rosa Mountains and stretched across a parched area of semi desert, another group of rises in the northeast.

"More smoke that could mean we'll be playin' with fire, man," Joe Straw growled to break the silence that had held between them since they left the stream.

"Take it easy, Joe," Edge answered easily. "And remember I know where you hurt the most."

"You know one of the easiest things to say to somebody, Edge? It's don't worry. But it's one of the hardest things for the person being told to do."

"Live for the day, feller. Tomorrow never comes."

"So I say some stupid things sometimes. Sometimes a man has cause to worry. I'd be a whole lot happier if we rode around that place ahead."

He and Edge had not shifted their gaze from

the building since it first emerged from the shimmering heat haze, and they studied each new detail of the composite whole as it came into clear view.

There were two buildings, side by side with a gateway between them, an empty corral out back of them, a well out front of the nearest one which had the stone chimney climbing up the frame end wall. This building had a stoop with a water trough in front of it. Four horses with saddles on their backs were hitched to a rail that ran across the top of the trough.

When he had seen all of this, Joe Straw turned to show his anxiously frowning face to Edge who rode ten feet behind the gelding.

"Four horses, man."

"I can count."

"Chances are four men."

"Go along with that."

"Breed hatin' white men. And me a half Comanche and you a half Mexican."

"On the other hand, Joe. Four sisters of mercy came out here to see that we minorities are being treated right."

"Up a pig's ass, man. You just said—"

Edge took out the makings and spat at the side of the trail as he began to roll a cigarette. Then he grinned at the apprehensive man riding ahead of him.

"Just giving a happy-go-lucky feller like you the bright side to look on, Joe. I always view the other side. So sometimes I get a pleasant surprise. Most times I'm not disappointed. Just keep on riding slow and easy. And do what I tell you when I tell you."

"Easy for you to say when you got a handgun and a rifle and a—"

"First thing I have to tell you is to keep your mouth shut, Joe."

Straw glowered at Edge, who ignored him as he lit the cigarette and continued to concentrate his attention on the way station and its surroundings.

He was close enough to see that it was built at an intersection of trails, for one spurred off to the left, and curved into the fold between two hills to the west. Closer still, he could guess that the four horses at the trough had been ridden along the west trail to get to the way station. The geldings were in good shape, showing no signs of recent long travel. Edge knew it was a long way to anywhere on the south trail and he could see there was nothing across the desert until the distant hills.

The two riders and the mule were within four hundred feet of the building with the chimney on the side when a man began to sing. Forcing the words in a gravel tone, off key and out of tune, "Oh give me a home where the buffalo roam where the deer and the antelope—"

"Sing it louder, mister!" a young man yelled. "Yeah, and put more damn feelin' into it, why don't you?"

Another youngster said, "Like you was singin' a love song to this pretty little wife you got, Mr. Ford!"

"Hey, that'd be even better! Ask him if he knows any pretty love songs to sing, Clyde!"

"Aw shit, man, I told you there'd be trouble," Joe Straw whined.

70

"The mouth, Joe," Edge reminded.

"What?"

"Told you to keep it shut."

"Ask him yourself, Ward!" Clyde snapped. "I'm busy! Set them up again, Mrs. Ford. All round. Include you and your sweet singin' husband, ma'am."

"He ain't singin' sweet or any other friggin' way, Clyde."

"Watch your friggin' language, Sonny! There's a friggin' lady present."

"That's no friggin' lady, Clyde," Sonny countered. "That's his wife!"

A gust of drunken laughter greeted the joke and when Joe Straw glanced over his shoulder to show an expression of anguished pleading, Edge cracked a cold grin.

He said, "They sound like your kind of people, feller. A barrel of laughs."

They were close to the buildings and could smell the aroma of food cooking mixed in with the woodsmoke from the chimney. They were able to read the weather-faded sign painted on a plank fixed above the doorway and flanking windows in the morning shade of the stoop.

TRANS-TERRITORIAL STAGE LINE
WAY STATION NO. 3

Edge nodded for Straw to angle off the trail past the well and toward the hitching rail above the trough.

"Please boys!" an older man implored. "You've had your fun and—"

"You was told to sing!" Clyde was no longer a happy drunk. Sullen anger had taken command of his mood. "So friggin' sing!"

He emphasized the order with a smash of breaking glass.

Mrs. Ford screamed.

Ward yelled, "Hey, that's a waste of good liquor, buddy!"

"There's plenty here!" Sonny countered, his high humor unabated. "Come on, Mr. Ford! Sing up! The friggin' party's still goin', ain't it?"

"If it ain't, I reckon the lady here could get it started again!" the unnamed youngster announced gleefully. "By sheddin' a little of the threads she's wearin'! What d'you say, Clyde?"

"Sure is kinda hot in here, Dave!" His mood had changed again and there was a leer in his voice now. "Mrs. Ford oughta be more comfortable if she didn't have so much—"

"Clyde, I don't think we oughta let this get outta hand!" Ward cut in, speaking quickly and nervously.

"Please, boys!" Ford tried again. "You can't mean you'd—"

"Sing, you snivellin' little corward!" Clyde roared. And this time he punctuated his command with a gunshot that forced another scream from the woman and a howl from her husband.

Edge and Straw swung from their saddles after halting the mare and the gelding at the trough alongside the four horses already hitched there. Straw froze with the hand of his good arm fisted to the horn and one foot in the stirrup, his green, fear-filled eyes fixed upon the impassive face of his captor.

Edge signalled with one hand for the man to get off his horse, while the other slid the Winchester from the boot.

"Gi . . . give me . . . a . . . ho . . . me where the . . ."

"Start with the undressin', Mrs. Ford."

"You can't mean it?" the woman asked tearfully of Clyde.

". . . buffalo roam . . ."

Edge hitched the reins of his and Straw's mounts to the rail.

The mule stood in blank-eyed docility to the side.

"Oh, dear God help us," Ford pleaded.

"He sings and you strip off, lady!" Clyde said with cold menace. "Or Ward and Sonny hold him while Dave strips the clothes off you. Up to the both of you."

The highly charged exchange masked the sounds of the newcomers's arrival, dismount, and their footfalls on the hard-packed area fronting the way station. The tense silence which followed Clyde's ultimation was broken by the footfalls of Straw and Edge as they stepped up onto the stoop.

They drew every pair of eyes to the open doorway, the various expressions they had held an instant previously abruptly altered to incredulity. At the sight of the quaking half-breed Comanche with a limply hanging left arm, and the taller man without expression who stood at his side, a rifle canted to his left shoulder.

"We was just havin' a little harmless fun," one of the young men blurted huskily. He was Ward.

"Thank God you've come!" Ford forced out in a harsh whisper.

His wife breathed out, "Oh," and looked on the verge of fainting.

The kid who was as nervous as Ward was Sonny.

It was Dave who snarled, "They ain't no problem, Clyde!"

Clyde answered; "So you deal with them, buddy."

Dave found his gaze locked on the unblinking, narrow-eyed stare of Edge which had shifted around the room to briefly study each occupant in turn. Dave was suddenly afraid as Ward, Sonny, and Straw. His Adam's apple bobbed.

Then Edge took the cigarette from his mouth and pursed his lips. He asked evenly, "Obliged if somebody could tell me when the next northbound stage coach is scheduled."

Ford gasped.

His wife shook her head violently, as if attempting to physically rid her stunned mind of an image of reality she could not believe.

Straw's confidence returned in relation to the degree by which fear spread among three of the four youngsters, and he was unable to prevent a short, harsh laugh from bursting from his throat.

"It's late already," Clyde said sourly.

Edge nodded and hung the cigarette back at a corner of his mouth, and stabbed a long forefinger at Dave.

"No big deal for me, kid," he drawled. "If you want to be like the stage coach."

The youngster swallowed hard, "Uh?"

"Late."

Chapter Seven

"Uh?" Dave grunted again.

"Late means dead, stupid," Clyde growled and turned his back on the doorway to grab a bottle of rye and tilt it and his head to suck from the neck.

The public room of the way station was forty by forty with a counter running along the length of the side wall to the left of the doorway. A large cooking range was set into an alcove on the facing wall. Three steaming pots on top gave off appetizing aromas. Two trestle tables pushed together and flanked by backless bench seats were in front of the rear wall. There were two Boston rockers facing the windows to either side of the doorway.

Midway along the counter there was a gap barred by a closed flap. This break divided it into a bar and a store counter.

The tall, good looking, slenderly built, forty-year old blonde Mrs. Ford was behind the bar in back of her three shelves aligned with glasses and bottles of liquor and beer.

Dave was closest to her.

The woman's husband was in the store section,

between the counter and a half dozen shelves stacked with packages and cans and jars of provisions. He was ten years her senior with a fleshy face and flabby body with a circle of mottled gray hair on his otherwise bald skull.

Ward and Sonny were near him in front of the counter.

Clyde sat on the end of the bench close to the bar section.

All the youngsters were in their early twenties. Tall and lithe, sun-tanned and clean shaven. They were dressed like cowpunchers, which bore out the hunch Edge had when he saw the style of saddles and the kind of accoutrements which were on the horses hitched to the rail.

"Sisters of mercy, shit," Straw rasped.

Edge folded his forefinger back into the fist of his right hand, lowered the hand, and drove a jabbing blow into the small of the half-breed Comanche's back.

With a cry that was more alarm than pain, Straw was sent staggering across the threshold.

Ward and Sonny scuttled nervously along the dual purpose counter to close with the scowling Dave.

"I tell you to speak, Joe?" Edge asked evenly when Straw pulled up from the involuntary move and swung around to glower his hatred at the rifle toting man in the doorway.

"That was outside, man!" He sank into a half crouch as if preparing to lunge back at Edge. "I swear I'll—"

Edge stepped into the way station and again all eyes were fixed on him. "Swear is like late, feller. Has more than one meaning. Don't like to hear dirty words in front of a lady. And it seems you can't talk without using them."

"Kate's heard worse than that, mister," the dripping with sweat Ford put in quickly. "Get you anythin' while you wait for the stage?"

"We got all we need." He gestured with a hand for Straw to sit on one of the rockers. "A place to rest out of the sun."

Straw complied sullenly with the tacit order and Edge dropped into the nearby chair after turning it so that he could survey the room. He rested the Winchester across his thighs, his hand fisted to the frame and muzzle aimed across the room.

"All right I leave, mister?" Kate Ford asked tentatively, and ran a sleeve of her shapeless brown dress over her sheened forehead, then finger combed her hair. "Just to our private rooms. I need to wash up. I ain't never felt so dirty."

She shot a glance of loathing toward the quartet of young cowpunchers.

"Your place, ma'am. You got the right to do what you want."

There was an arch between the shelves of the bar and the store section and she turned and hurried through it. She avoided meeting the gaze of her husband, filled with distress close to the point of tears.

Dave, who had a shot of black curly hair on the back of which his white Stetson was jammed, had taken his glass of whiskey when he retreated to where Clyde sat. In the tense silence after the woman's exit, the sound of the gulp when he swallowed the liquor was very loud.

Ward, who was the leanest of the four and

Sonny, who had the most bloodshot eyes, looked longingly along the counter to where their newly-filled glasses had been left in front of Ford.

"All right for me to talk now, man?" Straw asked.

"No sweat, Joe."

But Clyde spoke first. He swung a leg to straddle the end of the bench and growled with a sneer firmly set into his lean features, "Rather you didn't, mister. Seein' and smellin' the stink of him is bad enough. Don't want to hear him, too. Him being a no-good half breed."

He raised the bottle and tilted his head back to take another swig of rye.

Edge thumbed back the hammer of the rifle, elevated the barrel, and steadied the stock with his free hand, and squeezed the trigger.

A chorus of yells merged with the report of the gunshot. Then came the crash of smashing glass as the bullet blew the bottle into myriad pieces that were scattered amid the spraying liquor across the trestle table and floor. It mingled with the fragmented shards and pools of whiskey scattered by the bottle that Clyde had broken earlier.

"Son of a bitch!" Clyde roared, snatched his hand down from his mouth and hurled the undamaged neck of the bottle away. He powered to his feet to start with fear and rage at Edge who was pumping the lever action of the Winchester. "What'd I say, damnit? You ain't been treatin' him like he's some big buddy of yours, mister!"

Now Edge took the cigarette from his lips, dropped it to the floor and stepped on it. "He ain't. Took exception to you calling him a half-

78

breed, feller. Maybe would have even if I wasn't one myself."

"But he's got Indian in him, mister! You got the look of a Mex is all."

"Mexican."

"What?"

"Take exception to my Pa being called a Mex. I figure it the same as greaser."

"And you guys better not aim a gun at him without pulling the trigger," Straw said with the trace of an evil smile. "He takes exception to—"

"Obliged, Joe. Saves me from giving them the warning."

Clyde sank back into his straddle of the bench and dabbed with his kerchief at a small cut a piece of flying bottle glass had inscribed along his right cheek. The fear had left him now, but the anger still smoldered in his dark eyes. Dave, Sonny, and Ward looked at him apprehensively.

"He's your prisoner, ain't he?" Ford asked tentatively. "You're the law, I guess?"

"Only to himself, man," Straw growled.

Edge rocked his chair gently back and forth and did not shift his steady gaze away from the four youngsters across the room. He asked, "How late's the state coach, feller?"

Ford dug a watch out of a pocket of his vest and flipped open the lid. "Past eleven now, sir. Should've been through at ten."

"Where from and to?"

"She starts at Tucson and swings way down to the southwest before headin' north up through here. Then straightaway almost to Phoenix. Long distance, and it ain't unusual for her to be late.

79

Same with the southbound, but that ain't so bad, of course, on account of—"

"Phoenix will be fine, feller. How far across the territorial line to Crater, Joe?"

Ford had been dividing his nervous attention between the quartet of men at the rear of the room and the two by the window at the front. He talked fast and seemed set to go on for hours as if he felt that the sound of his voice chattering about inconsequentials was capable of diminishing the tension in the stove-heated room.

"Find your own way, man! I ain't about to help you get me up there so I can . . ."

Straw let the sentence hang unfinished, as anxious about the four young cowpunchers as was Ford. The switch from scowling defiance was caused by the manner in which Clyde suddenly stood up and swung away from the bench.

"Hell, Mr. Ford, I'm real sorry for the hell we was raisin' just now. We all are. You know that weren't like us."

The flabby man behind the counter was as distrustful as Edge and Straw at the totally unexpected apology. Then Clyde dropped his look of contrition for a second to glower at his equally startled companions, who nodded hurriedly, without losing their expressions of bewilderment.

"It was the liquor that did it. And us being ready for some hair to be let down after four solid months of nothin' but work and sleep out on the Santa Rosa spread. We went too far, we know that. But it wouldn't't've gone any further."

"That's right, Mr. Ford," Ward added quickly. "I was already tellin' them to knock it off, wasn't I?

You heard me. They'd have listened. Drunk as we all were."

Clyde delved a hand into a hip pocket and came out with a ten dollar bill. "Here," he offered as he approached the suspiciously frowning Ford. "Take this. More than covers the cost of the liquor. Buy your wife somethin' nice. From us. To make up for the bad time we give her."

With his free hand, hidden behind his back, Clyde made a frantic gesture for the other three cowpunchers to head for the doorway.

"Okay, boys," Ford said with a sweating faced smile. "Apologies accepted. You was always nice to me and Kate when you used the place for tobacco and liquor to go in the past. I was young and high spirited myself awhile back."

Ford reached out with his right hand to take the bill that was extended by Clyde's left.

Straw rasped. "This is wrong, man," and he flashed his green-eyed stare from the apparently indifferent Edge to the three young men who were almost at the doorway.

"Don't shoot unless you have to."

The softly spoken words drew every pair of eyes toward the speaker. Then they shifted to look at the point in the room which held the unemotional attention of Edge. They were staring fixedly at the archway behind the counter as Kate Ford stepped slowly through it, an old .54 bore Tranter percussion revolver held rock steady in front of her face in a double-handed grip. She aimed at Clyde's head over a range of six feet, that closed to three before she halted.

Clyde was like a carved statue, but unlike a

81

statue, he had pores in his haggard face that oozed sweatbeads.

Dave, Ward, and Sonny had frozen just as rigidly at the side of the rocker in which Straw sat. The right hand of each man was held close to his holstered Colt Army Model, fingers bent at the start of a curl for a draw.

"You better give me a good reason not to, mister," the savagely grimacing woman said, her tone hard as granite.

"Nice sunny day outside, ma'am. And I figure it would make it for you to blow out his brains. But there'll be a whole lot of dark nights when it won't be the fault of the cold you'll wake up trembling."

"The man's right, Kate," her husband forced out hoarsely between quaking lips.

Clyde turned his head to stare along the barrel of the big old Tranter and into the face of the woman behind the gun. And to his terror-filled eyes, it seemed that the oiled gun metal and the sweat tacky flesh were constructed of materials of equal hardness.

"Please, ma'am," he croacked.

"Clyde, tell us!" Dave pleaded helplessly as he raked his eyes from his friend at the counter, those at his sides, and Edge.

"Get out," Clyde ordered, intending it to be a snarled order. But the words emerged from his fear-constricted throat in the tone of an imploring whisper. "Get out and don't try nothin'."

"Sure, Clyde. Sure. Come on you guys," said Ward, who started across the threshold, tugging at Sonny's shirt sleeve.

Sonny submitted to the urging, but Dave remained where he was, his right hand still close to the holstered gun. Doubt was deeply inscribed on the tanned flesh of his face.

"The lady's still making up her mind, feller," Edge said. "My decision's made. Two steps 'll take you through the doorway. After three seconds you'll have to be carried out."

Dave raked his gaze toward Edge and saw the aim of the Winchester had been altered. The stockplate of the rifle was resting against the base of the man's flat belly and the barrel was angled upwards, the muzzle in line with Dave's heart.

The frightened Joe Straw was leaning far to the side of the rocker on which he sat, green eyes constantly flicking along their sockets to glance at Edge and Dave, sweatingly conscious of being trapped in a crossfire situation. He was safe from Edge's steadily aimed rifle, but what if the cowpuncher got his gun clear of the holster and cocked before he was hit?

"Do it, for God's sake!" Clyde rasped.

"Or you both get dead together!" Kate Ford snarled.

Dave did not so much stride from the way station as leap, the thud of his booted feet on the stoop sounding in unison with a curse of frustrated rage.

Straw straightened in his chair and jutted out his lower lip to direct a draught of cool air over his face. "Man, oh man," he sighed.

"They done like you wanted," Clyde said.

His left hand was still extended, proffering the ten spot.

With a grin of relief mixed with triumph, Ford snatched it from the hand, dropped the bill on the countertop, and reached cautiously forward to ease the Colt out of Clyde's holster.

"Didn't appreciate your custom, mister, so ain't gonna say come back."

It was as if Clyde was oblivious to everything in his fear-filled world except the unblinking, un-flinching, blank-eyed face of the woman.

She said, "I oughta have you strip yourself naked, boy. Then make you sing. Soprano. After I've cut off your balls."

"Kate!" her husband blurted, the grin wiped from his fleshy face.

"Don't worry, Fred. I'm still thinkin' about them long, dark nights the stranger spoke of. Go join your friends, boy."

Clyde seemed incapable of moving for a second. Then, slowly he turned and started toward the doorway. For three-quarters of the way, he kept his head screwed around, holding his breath as he stared at the woman who tracked him with the gun in the double-handed grip.

Then Straw said bitterly, "If you hadn't run off at mouth about breeds, man, I could maybe have helped to end this differently."

Clyde allowed the pent up breath to rush from between his teeth. His dark eyes lost their look of fear, and were soon glittering with hatred, which he directed fully at Edge after just a momentary glance at the half-breed Comanche.

"I'll remember you, mister," he spat.

"Lot of people say I've the most unforgettable character they ever met, feller."

Edge came up from the chair and in two strides was on the threshold a second after Clyde crossed it out of line of fire of the woman's Tranter.

The Winchester was canted to his left shoulder and his right hand hovered close to the butt of the Colt jutting from the holster.

Dave, Ward, and Sonny were standing in a disconsolate group by the water trough. Their eyes raked from the glowering Clyde to the man in the doorway. They were ready to be afraid again. But Clyde, when he joined them and started to unhitch his horse, was merely smolderingly defiant.

"Mount up," he growled.

He swung into his saddle and waited for the other three to follow his example. Each man had a Winchester jutting from a forward hung boot.

"If nothin' else, you son of a bitch," Clyde hissed, "you done us outta ridin' the stage coach. And after four months range ridin' with these friggin' nags under us, we're gonna hate you more everytime we got a new blister on our asses."

"Give you a chance to find out what kind of buddies you are to each other."

"Ain't none closer," Ward said vehemently.

Edge nodded. "When a feller needs tending in that area, he finds out who is real friends are."

They thudded their spurs into the flanks of their mounts and galloped out onto the trail to ride north ahead of a long cloud of dust. The mule set off after them.

Edge swung around on the threshold of the way station and saw that Joe Straw had risen from the rocker, gone to the counter, and picked up the full shot glasses left there by Ward and Sonny.

His good looking face was spread with a broad grin while he ignored the less menacingly aimed gun in Kate Ford's grip and the uneasy Fred Ford.

"They been bought and paid for, man," the half-breed Comanche reminded. "I figure enough good liquor's been wasted already. One each, uh?"

Edge approached him and took one of the glasses from Straw as the man flinched away from him. "Never do drink hard liquor before noon, Joe."

Behind the grin, Straw was nervously unsure of what his captor's reaction would be. And he quickly raised the hand of his good arm to toss the rye against the back of his throat. Then he set the glass down on the counter.

Edge handed him back the other one, and he sipped this drink, relishing the taste of the whiskey. He was certain now that this privilege was not part of some cruel trick.

With a sigh of relief, Kate Ford set the revolver down on the countertop as the tension drained out of her.

Her husband snatched up the gun and stowed it under the counter, out of reach of Straw. Then he looked at Edge with an expression of heartfelt gratitude.

"Is there anythin' I can get you, mister? If there is, it's on the house. But it won't be enough to thank you for gettin' rid of them drunken bums before somethin' really bad happened to me and Kate."

Edge shook his head.

"He don't take kindly to being thanked, man. But if it wasn't for me, he wouldn't have been here most likely. And I sure as hell wouldn't say no to a bottle of this fine whiskey."

He looked eagerly from Ford to Edge and back again.

Edge placed a dollar bill on the countertop. "Two plates of whatever's cooking, feller. I'll buy it." He jerked a thumb at Straw. "If you want to give him a bottle of rye, that's up to you."

With a shrug, Ford moved along behind the counter to the bar section, took a bottle from the shelf there, and brought it back to get it down in front of the half-breed Comanche, who swallowed what remained in the glass and then sprayed some of the liquor out again as a short laugh exploded from his throat when he fisted a hand around the bottle.

"Man, we're friends for life!" he blurted.

Edge pursed his lips, then drew them back to display a thin line of his teeth in an ice cold smile. "That's fine with me, Joe," he drawled. "It's the only kind of friendships I get into."

"What's that, man?" Straw asked happily as he poured himself a fresh drink.

"Short ones."

Chapter Eight

Joe Straw did not want any of the stew and potatoes that Kate Ford ladled onto plates and set down on the trestle table between the two men seated opposite each other.

So Edge ate two helpings while his prisoner drank glass after glass of rye whiskey. The woman completed cleaning up the mess made by the broken bottles before going back into the way station's private quarters.

Fred Ford was out in the stable, feeding and currying the mare and the gelding, from time to time casting anxious glances along the north trail, fearful the four cowpunchers might return to seek revenge for their humiliation. They had been swallowed by the shimmering heat haze and not a living thing could be seen moving on the desert. After awhile, the overweight way station manager began to make frequent surveys on the trail that ran out of the Santa Rosa Mountains. He was eager for the delayed stage coach to arrive so that he could be rid of the taciturn half-breed Mexican and his volatile part Indian prisoner.

He was sure, now that he had time for calm thinking, that they were a highly dangerous combination, not intending any harm to Kate and himself, maybe. If the fuse happened to be lit, there was no guarantee that innocent bystanders would not be hurt in the inevitable explosion, so best that he be aboard the stage coach lost in the heat shimmer or even further away from here.

In the way station, Joe Straw said with an air of profundity, "You're not such a bad guy, you know that man? That kid sheriff wouldn't have allowed me no whiskey, that's for sure."

He was halfway into the bottle and had now dispensed with the glass, sucking the whiskey from the neck. He was already a lot drunker than the cowpunchers had been, a fixed grin on his face, but this was abruptly curtailed and replaced by a look of bitterness.

"I should've killed that bastard when I had the chance."

"You did, Joe."

He shook his head. "No, when I got away from him. I tell you how I did that already?"

"No, feller."

"Middle of the night it was, man. We was camped by this arroyo. Him snorin' like a hog. Me with my ankles tied and my hands tied behind my back. Hurtin' like hell from being' tussed up that way for so long. But figurin' how to get loose. Then a stick fell outta the fire. Red, glowin' hot. Swung my legs around and put the rope to the stick. Had to kick a few more sticks loose before the rope was burned through."

He grinned at the remembered pleasure of

success and took a long swallow of whiskey.

"Lot harder to burn through the rope around my wrists, man. Had to work blind. And it cost me." He turned his hand holding the bottle so that Edge was able to see the scars of recent burning on the inside of his wrist. "Same on the other one, man. And I couldn't even yell out in case it woke Hackman."

"Brave and smart, Joe."

Straw shook his head. "It was smart to figure out the idea with the sticks, but then I acted dumb. Instead of sneakin' up on Hackman and gettin' his rifle or revolver, I went the other way to where the horses were hitched, saddled mine and led him away real quiet two miles maybe before I mounted up and rode like a bat outta hell."

Another hefty slug from the bottle gave a slur to his voice. "Should've got one of his guns and killed him, Edge. Instead of runnin' off the way I did. Leavin' him alive to come after me. Real dumb, man."

Edge waited until more whiskey tipped down his throat before saying, "Or stuck him with the knife, Joe."

The liquor-glazed and bloodshot eyes blinked across the table. "What, man?"

"The knife you had hidden in the crease of your ass, feller."

The eyes briefly revealed that the half-breed Comanche was troubled by the comment, which had not so much reminded him of anything—instead had brought to the surface something he preferred to remain buried. Then the tell-tale expression was gone and he took the heftiest yet drink from the bottle. He left a quarter-inch of whiskey in the bottom.

Now he directed a challenging look into the impassive face of his captor. "So all right, man! And I wouldn't've had to get close to do that! I could throw that knife better than most guys can shoot a pistol!"

He drained the bottle dry and waved it in the air. "You figure we helped them enough to deserve another?"

"I know you did," Kate Ford announced on cue, as she emerged from the archway, her face freshly washed and her hair neatly combed, wearing a white dress that hugged her torso more closely than the previous one. "And it's after midday now."

She raised the central flap to bring the bottle out from behind the counter, her madeup eyes asking tacit permission of Edge.

He nodded and as she set the bottle down on the table, he laid a five dollar bill beside it.

Straw grabbed the bottle and removed the stopper with his teeth.

"You really are a most difficult man to express gratitude to, Mr. Edge," she accused reproachfully.

"You got the drop on him, ma'am. I just happened to be around."

"That's not the point, surely. Fred and me would have been in bad trouble if you had not been around. All I want to do is to show my appreciation."

"You wanna drink, man?" Straw slurred after

taking his first long swallow from the new bottle.

"No, Joe." He shifted his gaze briefly to Kate Ford as the woman picked up the two dirty plates and eating irons. Her once pretty face had been hardened and aged by living on the harsh frontier but there was a basic sensuality about the cast of her features that was more carnally attractive than mere feminine good looks. And she had taken care of her lithe, high-breasted body. She sensed his glancing survey and met his eyes, glinting slits of blue under hooded lids. "If it wasn't for Fred, maybe you could, ma'am," he said.

Now she smiled without coyness, with something close to pride and appreciation of his unveiled compliment.

Then her husband re-entered the way station's public room by the front door and she blushed guiltily and kept her face averted from him when she hurried back through the arch with the dirty dishes.

"No sign of the northbound yet," Fred announced. And remained on the threshold, his back to the room, as he filled and lit a pipe.

Edge rolled and lit a cigarette. And reflected without regret upon all his women before Beth and after her. There had not been many for a man of his age who had drifted over such vast distances, but then there had been more than a grain of truth in his earlier cynical comment to Joe Straw about preferring short friendships.

Preferring them, hell. He had to curtail any relationship that involved love for a woman or regard for a man or have it blasted asunder by the violent actions of others.

"You've figured me out, ain't you man?" the half-breed Comanche slurred in a maudlin tone, cutting into Edge's fresh memories of a woman named Crystal Dickens. "You've filled me up with liquor to find out the friggin' truth about me."

Straw was swaying gently from side to side, his green eyes half-closed and his mouth slack.

"I have, Joe?"

"Sure you have, you rotten shit. But I don't give a frig. In a pig's ass do I give a shit. But there's somethin' I want you to know, man. I sure as hell did sell my squaw of a mother down in Sonora."

Fred Ford snapped his head around to stare with shock, then contempt at the drunken half-breed Comanche who was hunched on the bench seat, his back to the room.

"Did I hear him right, mister?"

Despite his liquor dulled senses, Straw heard the man. He made to swing around to grin at him, but was in danger of toppling to the floor, so he abandoned the attempt.

"You sure did, man. And you know what I think? I think this bounty hunter here is set on seein' me hung because of that. And you know why I think that, man?" He paused, looking puzzled, as he lost the thread of what he was saying. He took another swig from the bottle and grinned again. "Now I remember! He's hard as rock on the outside, but toasted marshmallow inside, man. He don't give a shit that I held up the stagecoach and blasted the dumb driver's head off. And stuck that kid lawman with a knife. On account of he knows it was their own stupid fault they got dead."

"He makin' the kinda sense I think he is with all this crazy talk, mister?" Ford asked.

"They say a drunk man always tells the truth, feller," Edge answered. "Know he killed two men. Way he keeps telling about selling his Ma, I figure it happened like he tells it."

Straw refused to release his hold around the neck of the bottle. He lowered it gently to the table and unfolded his forefinger to point at Edge as his grin became one of triumph. "Ah, but I ain't no natural born killer like somebody I know, man! Am I? I ain't never killed nobody before. Old man Hackman, it was him or me."

His green eyes clouded over and a tear squeezed from the corner of each and ran down his sweat greasy cheeks. "And it was a bad time for me afterwards, man. What you said to the woman here is right. Somebody who ain't a killer, they pay real bad . . ." Still gripping the bottle, he used the back of his hand to wipe the tears from his cheeks. "And that kid sheriff, man. That was self defense, too. It was either the knife in his guts or a rope around my neck. And the son of a bitch kept comin' after me, didn't he? If I was a natural born killer, I'd have stuck him when I got away from him, wouldn't I? Or sneaked one of his guns and shot him while he was asleep. But I couldn't friggin' do that. And look where it's got me?"

He tilted back his head, raised the bottle, and sucked in the liquor with the greed of a dehydrated man getting his first drink of water after long days in an arid desert while the tears ran down his cheeks unchecked.

It had the inevitable effect—the bottle was not quite drained dry before this fresh intake of raw whiskey attacked his brain that was already dulled by earlier indulgence. So he passed out. He would have crashed backwards off the seat and onto the floor had not Edge reached across the table with both hands, one to fist around the bottle and the other to catch hold of one side of the Comanche waistcoat.

He set the bottle down on the table and eased the unconscious man gently forward to prevent him falling, slumped his head, torso, and good arm across the table.

"He sounds like he's ashamed of havin' decent feelin's mister," Fred Ford muttered with a shake of his head. "And yet proud of sellin' his own mother."

"Everybody's different, feller," Edge answered as he rose to go around to the other side of the table. "No matter how much they try to be like somebody else."

The pipe smoking way station manager caught his breath when he saw Edge take the straight razor from the neck pouch. He was merely intrigued as he watched the man use it to cut away the blanket binding around Straw's upper left arm.

The half-breed Comanche was lucky. The entry and exit wounds were clean of poison and the arm was not swollen to suggest internal infection from dirt or a dislodged piece of bone. The punctured flesh was puckered and looked sore, that was all.

"We got salve and bandages in stock, mister."

"He'll be okay without."

Edge got his Winchester from against the wall

and went to the doorway. Ford backed out in front of him.

"Sellin' your own mother. That's terrible." Ford's fleshy face wore an expression that came close to being of physical pain. "God, he deserves to be hanged for that."

Edge arched his cigarette into the water trough. "That's what he thinks I think, feller."

"And don't you, mister?"

"No. I figure it's the only thing he ever did in his life that's in keeping with the kind of feller he'd like to be."

"Like you?" Ford swallowed hard and gazed apprehensively at Edge, afraid he may have overstepped the mark.

"Maybe," was the quiet, evenly spoken response.

"You mean you would . . ." the way station manager decided not to finish the query. Even though Edge's impressive expression did not alter to warn him against it.

"A man does what he has to. Even when I know all the circumstances, I never judge him unless he's planning to keep me from doing what I have to."

Ford shook his head. "That don't add up, mister. If he's done all you and him says he has, he deserves to be strung up, like I said. And you ain't the judge, nor the jury, nor the hangman. Not even a lawman, way I heard it. Yet you're takin' him back to be hung. And doin' your best to keep him alive so he'll swing, seems to me."

Edge sat down on the stoop, feet on the hard-packed area fronting the way station so that he could glance over his shoulder and see where the

97

deeply breathing Joe Straw was sprawled across the table at the rear of the room.

"There's a price on his head. What I have to do is collect it."

Ford blew out a stream of smoke with a sigh, then knocked the ash from his pipe on one of the hitching rail support posts.

"There's a whole lot better ways of makin' a dollar, mister. And seems to me you don't much enjoy the line of work you're in."

Kate Ford spoke from behind the counter, and revealed she had been there for some time. "Now you're makin' judgments, Fred. On a man who saved us from God knows what."

Her husband shook his head. "Ain't no denyin' that he done that, Kate. But it was just our good fortune them four drunks started to rile him. It wasn't on purpose he helped us. Right, mister?"

Edge was gazing out along the southern stretch of the trail into the mountains. He grunted softly when he was sure it was the stagecoach he could see in the distance. He answered, "Didn't have anything here I haven't paid for."

"With blood money, I'll be bound."

"You're bound to take it. It's the only kind I've got."

Now the older man saw the stage coach to south and growled, "Here she comes, Kate. I'll go get the fresh team."

There was angry contempt in his gait as he headed across the gateway of the corral and swung into the stable.

"I don't care what Fred says, mister," the woman said vehmently as Edge rose to his feet and she crossed to stir the pots of simmering food. "I give you full credit for—"

"Don't need it, Mrs. Ford," he interrupted. "Like I just told him. I've paid for everything I've had."

Chapter Nine

The ancient Concord was hauled off the trail and onto the area fronting the way station by a team of four weary horses and rolled to a halt with little raising of dust.

"You're real late today, Charlie!" Fred Ford called after the horses had stopped snorting and the timber and harness ceased to creak.

"On account of the dead we had to bury, Fred," the bearded, wrinkled old timer holding the reins answered sourly, and directed a stream of dust stained saliva at the ground.

"Dead?"

"Right, Fred," the clean shaven, old man riding shotgun supplied as he eased down from the seat ahead of the driver. "Three of them. Young sheriff with a knife in his belly and two guys looked like they was pros—"

"After seeing for myself, Mr. Dodds, I have no wish to listen to the gory details, if you please." She was perhaps ten years older than the driver and shotgun, who were in their early sixties. Her hair was grayer and her skin was more heavily marked with wrinkles. The scowl on her face as

101

she peered through wireframe spectacles and out of the open window of the stagecoach door, looked like it was a more or less a permanent fixture on her angular features. "Kindly let me out of this stagecoach so that I may rest and refresh myself."

Dodds muttered something under his breath that was probably a curse, but opened the door and offered a hand to help the old lady down from the Concord.

She was on the ground and two middle aged, soft looking men were emerging behind her when she caught sight of the figures at the way station doorway and gave vent to a squeal of alarm.

"Dear God in Heaven, another one!" she exclaimed shrilly as Dodds, the driver and her two fellow passengers saw what it was that had upset her: Edge, with the Winchester canted to his left shoulder and the unconscious Joe Straw slumped face down over the right one.

"Dead drunk is all he is, ma'am," came the reply as Edge stepped off the threshold from the stoop and carried his burden toward the stagecoach.

The group blocking the way to the open door parted to allow him through.

"And he is to be allowed to ride on the stagecoach?"

The driver and shotgun shuffled off in response to an urgent beckoning gesture of Fred Ford while the two male passengers hurriedly made for the way station. The old lady stayed where she was, head cocked to catch a glimpse of Straw's face.

"I'll be along to see he causes no trouble,

ma'am," Edge told her as he entered the Concord to deposit the oblivious Straw on a corner seat.

"I thought so! From the way he is dressed! That man is an Indian!"

"You're half right, ma'am. His Pa was Irish. You have something against Indians?"

"Certainly not! I am chairwoman of the Tucson Branch of the Red and White Association, young man. An organization founded to promote mutual understanding between the Indians and ourselves. And those of mixed blood are of special concern to us because they attract mistrust from both . . ." She broke off and stared hard at Edge. Then she demanded shrilly, "What are you doing to him?"

Edge had taken from his pants pocket a ball of twine borrowed from Kate Ford. Next he climbed aboard the Concord and sat down opposite Straw, leaned across, and began to bind the hands of the unconscious man together.

"I'm tying him up, ma'am."

"Why?"

"Because he's due to be hung, so he's anxious to escape."

"He's a criminal?"

"A killer."

"You are not a lawman?"

"No, ma'am."

She was perturbed by the revelations about Straw and tried to look more closely at the face of the half-breed Comanche—as if she felt it might show confirmation that what Edge said was true. She glimpsed his profile while his chin was slumped down onto his chest. So she gazed quizzically at Edge.

"You do not look like an officer of the courts. Such a man would hardly allow a prisoner to get passing out drunk," she nodded as the facts supplied the obvious answers to her rhetorical questions. Then she spoke more firmly, "That man has not been tried and convicted, has he? You are in the process of delivering him to the locality where he is alleged to have committed the crimes? For financial reward, no doubt?"

Edge had tied the knots. Now he sat back in his seat, took out an already rolled cigarette and struck a match. He used the flame to burn through the twine before he lit the cigarette. Then he replied, "That's exactly right, ma'am."

The woman nodded again and uttered a throaty grunt, "We have to deal with many cases of mistreatment to Indians by whites while the poor wretches are awaiting court proceedings, young man."

"It was his idea to get this drunk," Edge said as he climbed out of the stage and closed the door.

She grimaced. "If the man chooses to get into such a state, that is up to him. But for as long as we are to share this journey, I would ask that you observe his human rights. You should not prejudge the outcome of his trial and therefore you should treat him with dignity and—"

Edge, the Winchester canted to his shoulder, swung away from her and headed for the stable where Fred Ford was leading out the fresh team while Charlie and Dodds were putting the trail-weary horses into stalls.

The woman snorted her disgust, picked up the skirts of her severe black dress, and hurried into the way station, muttering under her breath.

"That's Mrs. Dora Naulty, mister," Charlie growled. "Always figured my wife for a talker, but that one . . ."

"She can run off at the mouth all she likes, so long as she ain't spoutin' orders at me," Dodds said sourly while Charlie was shaking his head.

"How long before stagecoach time?" Edge asked.

"Fifteen minutes at the most, mister," the bearded driver answered as he shot a sidelong glance at Edge. "We lost a lot of time buryin' those dead fellers because Mrs. Naulty told us we had to."

Edge was easing the black gelding and mare out of their stalls.

"Fred told me and Harry the halfbreed killed the lawman."

"Wasn't much of him left to put in the ground," the shotgun added. "Pretty torn up by the buzzards. Him and the horse both. The two old guys at the bottom of the cliff this side of the pass, they wasn't too—"

"I killed them," Edge supplied after checking the saddlebag to see that the stolen money was still there.

"You did?" Charlie said nervously.

"Them or me."

"Come on, Harry. Let's go grab a bite of Kate's grub."

They left the stable with several surreptitious glances at Edge, who ignored them as he put the reins on the two horses and then draped the saddles over their backs, but did not fasten the cinches.

He led them out into the bright sunlight,

hitched the reins to the rear of the Concord, and heaved the saddles and bedrolls up onto the roof among the baggage of the other three passengers. Then he climbed back into the stagecoach and sat down opposite the still oblivious Straw. He rested the stock of the Winchester on the floor and gripped the barrel between his thighs. He smoked the cigarette and waited patiently, listening to the deep and regular breathing of his prisoner and to the buzz of talk that filtered out through the way station doorway—this accompanied by the scraping of eating irons on tin plates. He allowed his mind free rein and was impassively content when memories of Crystal Dickens filled it.

She had been so unlike Beth, yet of all the women he had known since the death of his wife, she had impressed him the most. Impressed him as a possible replacement for Beth? Certainly for a long time she saw herself as much. At Irving, Texas, and Ventura, Utah, and on the trail between them she had constantly tested him and made one compromise after another to become what she considered the kind of woman he wanted.

While he gave not an inch and in the process of losing her made her into a thief.

He hadn't thought about her at all as he rode south from Ventura and she headed north—he going nowhere and she intent upon returning to the familiar surroundings she left to search for him. He wondered if she got there. Was she able to spend the stolen money without any pangs of guilt? Thinking of it as no more than she deserved after what she had suffered by doing right by the wrong man.

There had been ample time to think about her as he rode the trail south, to the Mission of Santa Luiz were Apache violence erupted and there was little opportunity to reflect upon the past if a man wanted to stay alive and have a future.

From the mission to the head of the valley where he caught sight of Joe Straw? Another long, lone time when he could have done what he was doing now. And maybe he had. As he rode to Tucson and then out of town in another direction, his mind had been open to the vast store of his memories. But none had entered until Joe Straw questioned the kind of man he was, and the two prospectors triggered the memory of the woman by whom Edge judged all others.

Beth was gone forever and now that the time for grief was past he could experience only a dull ache of emptiness whenever he thought of her. This was self punishing and futile.

But should he not feel the same about Crystal? She was not dead, but the possibility of him ever seeing her again was very remote, as remote as the prospect of him ever changing from the man he had become. The kind of man that Joe Straw—a hapless killer by force of circumstances—seemed to admire.

Why did it matter? Why could he not sit aboard this stagecoach with the same peace of mind he had between Ventura and the head of the valley in the Santa Rosa Mountains? He was as emotionally untroubled as his implacable features suggested.

From the moment they met, Crystal Dickens

had no doubt about the kind of man he was. If she chose to become a thief in the final minutes before they parted that should not be his concern, provided she did not steal from him.

Who was the half-breed Comanche slumped in the seat across the Concord from him? He was just goods for sale, money on the hoof, and his price tag was the same whether he was delivered fresh for hanging or a stinking carcass for burial.

He ought to be able to consign the woman to that compartment of his mind reserved for memories of those who came before and after Beth. Joe Straw should mean no more to him than the two Scotsmen who he blasted to death and then tossed off the top of the cliff.

"All aboard, folks!" the bearded driver yelled as he emerged from the way station, and then bit off a wad of tobacco. He chewed some juice out of it before he shouted, "Stagecoach time!"

He crossed to the Concord and kept his watery eyes averted from the passengers already inside as he climbed up onto the seat.

The two soft looking men were first to respond to the call. Both were in their fifties, dressed in city suits complete with vests, their sole concession to the heat of the day seen in the way their bootlace ties were loosened beneath the unfastened top buttons of their shirts. One had gray hair showing under the brim of his Stetson, while the other, who wore a derby, had jet black hair. Both were clean shaven and were overweight for their five and a half feet tall frames.

They had not only eaten in the way station, but had taken the time to wash up and brush the trail dust from their clothing.

"Good day to you, sir," the gray-haired man greeted as he swung open the door and squeezed between the knees of Edge and Joe Straw. "I'm Dwight Tait. My partner is Franklin Carver. We are in the restaurant business in Phoenix. If you intend to hold over there, perhaps you will favor us with your custom?"

He sat down on the other end of the same seat as Edge, their backs to the front of the stagecoach. Carver nodded nervously to Edge and took the seat facing his partner.

Edge touched the brim of his hat and asked, "How long until we reach Phoenix?"

"Barring accidents, we should reach there by sundown tomorrow, sir."

"I never make plans that far ahead."

Harry Dodds and Dora Naulty came out of the way station, he staying close by her side and looking like he was ready to support her if she should stumble. She was pale faced, but looked able-bodied enough to get to the stage and climb aboard unaided. Dodds helped her up the steps anyway.

"Mr. Straw is in my seat, young man," she complained as the door was closed behind her. And the stagecoach tilted slightly as Dodds clambered up beside the driver.

"I'll move him, lady."

"That will not be necessary." She folded her slight frame on to the seat between Carver and the half-breed Comanche, removed her wide brimmed hat, and set it on her lap. "I am quite prepared to suffer discomfort if this poor wretch is to benefit."

Charlie creaked off the brakes, yelled at the

team, and cracked his whip above their backs. The horses, fresh from the confines of the stable and eager to take advantage of their limited freedom, responded at once and the stage jerked from its standstill.

On the way station stoop, Fred and Kate Ford raised their hands in farewell. The pipe smoking man expressed relief. His slim but solidly built wife directed her gaze solely at Edge and there was a degree of melancholy in her eyes.

Was she a victim of circumstances? She was living with her husband in this isolated situation because the course she had chosen to take down the years had led her into a trap from which there was no escape?

She was as much a prisoner as Joe Straw. Crystal Dickens had been confined to her New England home for so long by family ties.

Crystal had made her escape bid—and staked everything she possessed upon finding happiness with this made called Edge.

While Kate Ford, for just a couple of hours, had allowed her imagination to run through the possibilities of what life might be like if Edge and not her husband was the man who gave direction to that life.

Crystal suffered the reality. Kate Ford regretted that her fantasy could not become fact. Was Crystal happy now? Thanking her lucky stars that her relationship with Edge was at an end. Would Kate Ford soon look around her home and at her husband and reflect with a smile of quiet joy that she had much to be thankful for?

He shifted into a more comfortable position against the back of the seat and the side of the stagecoach as the sounds and movements of the Concord settled into a regular cadence after the jerking din of the start. He fastened his thoughts as well as his eyes on Joe Straw.

He was another victim of circumstances—a half-breed Indian viewed with contempt by almost everyone with whom he came into contact. What series of events had led him to sell his own mother into slavery? What kind of desperate straits had he been in when he held up the stagecoach and was forced to kill or be killed? He discovered he did not have what it took to kill his pursuer until he was in another trap from which the only escape was the ultimate act of violence.

If anyone should be a hard-bitten and embittered cold-hearted killer, surely it was Joe Straw, a half-breed outcast born as a result of rape, getting the shit kicked out of him all his life and simply suffering a different brand of humiliation on those infrequent occasions when the do-gooders like Mrs. Dora Naulty poured pity over him.

He knew what his harsh life should have made of him, but could not force himself to be anything he was not. And what he was not was a man like Edge.

He was another half-breed with Mexican instead of Comanche blood in his veins, but equally an object of scorn in the eyes of most pure blooded Mexicans and Americans. Here, though, the resemblance ended.

Edge enjoyed a happy family life during his childhood and youth until the War Between the States ended this period of his history. Tens of thousands of other young men went away to war and the vast majority of those fortunate enough to survive were able to return and rebuild a replica of what had once been.

It was unlikely that any came home to the brutal journey's end that awaited this one.

Riding this stagecoach along the dusty trail across the desert, Edge experienced no regret at having responded so brutally to the scene of violence he found at the Iowa farm so long ago. But the ice blue eyes that surveyed his prisoner from between the narrowed lids did lose a little of their glitter as he reflected upon the events which followed from the end of the trail of vengeance.

Events in which countless men and women had been caught up, hating him, indifferent to him, liking him and some—very few—loving him. Those whose lives were not ended by or because of him had been influenced by him.

How many for the better?

Perhaps there were some, but in his present mood he could not recall them unless he projected his thoughts into the realm of what may have happened had he not been at a particular place at a particular time. He was who he was and therefore where he was, as much a prisoner in his own life as everyone else, not by force of circumstances, though. By choice.

This was a gut twisting self admission to make for a man who enjoyed total freedom and paradoxically failed to enjoy it. He was capable of changing others by his example, for better or worse, and yet he remained constantly the same.

Because he had solely the need to stay alive. Did not *want* anything.

Joe Straw wanted to be as hard and mean as his experiences should have made him.

Kate Ford wanted more out of life than meeting the needs of her husband and passing through stage line passengers.

Her husband wanted no more customers who caused trouble.

Crystal Dickens wanted to be loved by Edge.

Clyde and his buddies wanted to let their hair down after four months of range riding.

Stewart and McBride wanted to be rich.

John Hackman wanted to avenge the death of his father.

His father wanted to protect the property of the passengers on the stagecoach he was driving.

And on this stage . . .

The driver and shotgun wanted to make up lost time.

The nervous partners in the Phoenix restaurant business wanted to be back in familiar surroundings after being away from home.

Mrs. Dora Naulty wanted whites and Indians to live in harmony together.

Edge pursed his lips and allowed a silent sigh to vent between them as he shifted his gaze to the monotonous panorama of the desert landscape passing the window.

By acknowledging this, where did it leave him? If all he needed was to stay alive, why was he riding this stage with the sole object of taking the hapless Joe Straw to the gallows? He could eat and drink and provide the other necessities for survival for a longtime to come on the bounty money he collected in Tucson. Before his stake was exhausted, there was surely a better than even chance of raising more money from a less hazardous chore than the one he had set himself when he rode toward rather than away from trouble at the head of the valley. A chore which would not have brought him into contact with the two prospectors and the four drunken cowhands. Joe Straw put his life on the line for as long as it took to reach Crater.

Maybe the half-breed Comanche was right, which brought him back to the paradox. He only needed to stay alive, and yet he did have a death wish. He could care nothing for those who had the misfortune to get caught in the no man's land of his emotional battlefield.

But no, this could not be right. If he cared nothing about them, why should his mind be troubled by the line of thinking that occupied him now?

The answer clicked into the forefront of his mind almost the instant after the query was posed. Two coincidences happening in a short space of time.

First there had been Crystal Dickens, who, if he had allowed her, might well have been able to work the same changes in him as Beth Day, but he rebuffed her every approach, simply used her as he used everyone else when he felt the need. He had been able to ignore her memory because he was well practiced in the art of forgetting everything which did not have a bearing on what held his attention in the present.

Secondly, John Hackman, who was riding the vengeance trail after the killing of his father, as long ago, Josiah C. Hedges had sought out the murderers of his kid brother.

This pair of parallels was too startling for his subconscious to absorb and kept deeply buried parallels with the only times in his life after the watershed of the war when he had wanted anything.

The love of a woman he loved, and revenge against those who had robbed him of someone he loved, were realized and in achieving them he experienced happiness and a sense of triumph.

Between Jamie and Beth and Beth and now . . . ? Hunger and thirst, heat and cold, weariness and pain. Discomfort, lust, his body and mind assaulted by the demands made upon every living thing if life is to be preserved. But in satisfying them he felt . . . nothing.

The answer was he had failed to recognize the emotion which troubled him because he had never experienced it before. Crystal Dickens and John Hackman by entering his life in such quick succession had triggered memories of automatic responses which were pleasant. From this had come the feeling he had never had before and which spread a grimace of disgust across his lean features.

Envy.

He envied what Joe Straw had felt when he twisted the knife in Hackman's belly after sinking it into the hilt, Kate Ford's attraction to him, and Fred Ford's ability to be happy running his way station in the middle of nowhere. He envied the singlemindedness of purpose that had kept Crystal Dickens searching for him and the determination with which she had sought to keep him, the way the cowpunchers were able to get drunk without thought of the consequences, the avarice of the prospectors, the revenge motive which kept John Hackman on the trail of Straw, old man

115

Hackman's readiness to die in the line of duty, and the simple desire of the other people aboard this stagecoach and the uncomplicated sense of satisfaction they would experience when they got what they wanted.

"I said, are you feeling quite well, young man?" Mrs Naulty snapped at Edge.

He shifted his unseeing gaze away from the desert terrain passing the window and glimpsed his hands which were fisted around the barrel of the Winchester. His knuckles were white from the tightness of his grip and now that he was aware of his surroundings he felt pain in his hands. Then he looked at the woman and glanced at Tait and Carver, who had interrupted a game of two-hand poker to eye him with the same degree of curiosity as Mrs. Naulty.

"Ma'am?"

"You are looking very pale."

Now he felt the tightness of the frown on his face and made a conscious effort to reshape his features into a grin. "Not green?"

"You feel sick, young man?" She showed concern and got to her feet. "I have a jar of sal volatile in my valise on the rack."

He shook his head. "Obliged, ma'am, but I ain't sick."

She arranged herself back into the prim and proper posture on the seat between Joe Straw and Franklin Carver as the poker game got under way again.

"Just troubled in the mind, it's my guess. And I'm pleased to hear it. Irrespective of how those men came to die in the mountains, you should have taken the trouble to bury them or at least covered them. As a matter of common decency."

Edge returned his gaze to what lay beyond the window and felt mild surprise at the degree to which the sun had slid down the south western section of the cloudless sky: at how long he had been locked in his private world of self-analysis. Soon it would be dusk, which meant he had passed most of the afternoon looking for an obvious answer that, when he found it, aroused self-anger, gone as quickly as it came.

"You cannot pretend you did not hear what I said then, young man!"

"I heard, ma'am."

"And have no answer?"

"Didn't hear any question."

"I was rather hoping you would offer some explanation for your barbaric behavior on the trail through the mountains, which I find difficult to reconcile with what the couple at the way station told me concerning how you assisted them."

"I don't understand myself sometimes, ma'am. Don't expect you to."

The stagecoach had been making steady progress across the desert, and now began to make a little more speed as the trail took a downgrade into a hollow.

"It is my experience that talking is often a great help when one is troubled."

Edge craned his head to look forward out of the window and saw that they were entering a shallow depression in the desert that extended for perhaps a mile. Then there was an upgrade flanked by outcrops of rock at the crest.

"Then you carry on, ma'am," he said as he

settled back in his seat, satisfied that the slight forward cant of the stagecoach would not cause Straw to tip off his seat.

Mrs. Naulty vented an unladylike grunt. "It is not I who am troubled, young man!"

"Sure you are, ma'am. Seems to me you're worried by what ails most every woman I've ever met."

"I beg your pardon?" She sounded ready to be insulted.

It was then, as Tait and Carver were unable to suppress an urge to laugh when Edge told her, "scared you're going to die before your mouth wears out."

Chapter Ten

The woman uttered a choked cry and then lapsed into glowering silence, sharing her tacit anger among the poker players who laughed and Edge for giving them the reason.

For several minutes there were terse exchanges between Tait and Carver as they played their no stakes game of five card draw to be heard above the thud of hooves and the creaking of harness and timbers.

Then Harry Dodds shouted, "What the hell is that, Charlie?"

"What the frig does it look like?" the driver snorted and brought the stagecoach to a halt.

There was nothing frenetic about the unscheduled stop, for the team was moving slowly as they hauled their burden up the final few yards of the grade. They had no time to get back to their regular cadence on the flat before the order was given to halt.

"A dead mule, Charlie."

"Real bright, Harry."

Two men showed on the rocks to either side of the stalled Concord, Clyde and Ward on the side where Edge and Joe Straw sat, Sonny and Dave opposite them. Each of them held a levelled Winchester with the hammer cocked and a forefinger to the trigger.

Sonny aimed his rifle at Franklin Carver. Ward covered Charlie. Dave had a bead on Harry Dodds and Clyde had his sights aligned on Edge.

"Nobody gets to die if everybody acts as bright as Harry!" the top man of the quartet of cowpunchers yelled.

"Dammit to hell, a hold up!" Dodds wailed in disbelief.

Charlie sounded far less perturbed than the man riding shotgun. "Unless we got some rich passengers, you boys are wasting your time," he said evenly.

"Figure we got more money than all of you people, old timer," Dave snarled.

"And we didn't get it by thievin'," Ward added.

Up on the seat, Charlie and Dodds had their arms raised high, the bearded driver moving his jaw rhythmically as he continued to chew on a plug of tobacco. He gazed sadly at the dead mule that was sprawled across the center of the trail with a bloodcrusted bullet hole between its eyes. The shotgun constantly swung his head to peer anxiously at the four young men with levelled rifles.

Inside the stage Tait and Carver sat in frozen attitudes, their gazes locked and their hands clawed to their thighs. The playing cards were scattered on the floor around their feet.

Dora Naulty had recovered from several moments of shock. It left her pale faced, but her bright eyes suggested her mind was clear and working smoothly. She had glanced at the men flanking the stalled stagecoach and then more rapidly at her fellow passengers. She decided Tait and Carver were as useless as the oblivious Joe Straw in terms of having an affect on what was going to happen next so she looked questioningly at Edge.

Edge in turn gazed impassively out of the window at Clyde—knowing it was this triumphantly smiling young cowpuncher with the aimed Winchester who would dictate what was to follow and he was prepared to adapt his plans to meet whatever course of action Edge elected to take.

Edge said and did nothing during the exchanges between the men outside the stage and the short silence that followed.

"Meant what I said, mister. We ain't killers."

"Unless you have to be, feller."

With the door window open, there was no need for either man to raise his voice.

"Don't have any quarrel with anyone aboard except you. If you start the lead flyin', no tellin' who'll get hurt."

Charlie spat tobacco juice between the rumps of the two rear team horses. "I got it. You boys are the ones who were givin' the Fords a hard time this morning'."

"Best you be as quiet as you're bright, old timer," Dave rasped.

Clyde expressed mild irritation. "What my buddy says applies to everyone. Quiet and still. Except for Edge. He's gonna step out of the stagecoach. Holdin' that rifle one handed by the bar-

121

rel. And with his other hand a long way from his holster."

Tait and Carver managed to unlock their stares and while Carver looked pleadingly out at Ward and Sonny, Tait said huskily, "You have to do as he says, sir. For the sake of the innocent."

Edge reached with his left hand to turn the handle and swing open the door while his right remained fisted around the barrel of the Winchester. He paused to glance at the terrified Tait and the gray-haired man was shaken by a momentary fit of trembling as he met the glinting eyes of Edge.

"You ain't got a rifle aimed at me, feller."

"What?"

"So you ain't got what it takes to give me orders."

He stepped onto the trail and now Clyde and Dave tracked him with their rifles. Edge held his matching Winchester out to the side, then lowered it to rest against the rear wheel of the Concord. He took two paces away and came to a halt directly beneath the rock where the pair of tense young men stood.

He was tense himself, beneath the surface impressions of calm that emanated with his expression and attitude. He was afraid of the menacing situation, but able to keep the fear in check as an ice cold emotion which would add determination and strength to whatever countermove he was able to make if an opportunity to retaliate came about.

Like everyone else, with the exception of Joe Straw, he was sweating. It was not so much the heat that squeezed salt beads from pores now.

The sun was already half hidden behind the distant southwestern horizon. The sky was crimson in that direction. Elsewhere, the brilliance had left the blueness of unclouded infinity. The first hint of the cold of night could be felt in the air.

Edge could see the eyes of Clyde and Dave looking down at him, and he sensed the almost palpable pressure against his rigid back as everyone else stared at him through the gathering dusk.

"Ease out the revolver and toss it away, mister," Clyde ordered. He grimaced as he failed to keep his nervousness from his voice.

Edge complied, holding the Frontier Colt with just the tips of his thumb and forefinger. When the gun thudded to the trail some ten feet from where Edge stood, Franklin Carver gasped, "Thank God."

"Now turn around and face the stagecoach, mister," Clyde snarled, over compensating for his anxiety.

"You are not going to—" The woman's voice was shrill with horror.

"Shut up!" Clyde roared, and triggered a shot from his Winchester.

The bullet went high into the darkening sky. And probably fell back to the arid desert before the sound of the shot ceased to ring in the ears of the frightened people on and around the stationery Concord.

"Do like he says, ma'am," Edge said evenly into the ensuing silence. "Never a good idea to rile a sore loser."

He completed the turn as he finished speaking the warning. He saw from the deeper fear that spread across the faces that he was just a moment away from getting what the cowpunchers thought he had coming to him.

He was wrongly positioned to see the shadows of Clyde and Ward. He heard one of them draw in a sharp breath, then the scape of boot leather against rock and the subdued whistling sound of something solid being swung through the air.

The rock upon which the two men stood was about four-feet high. Dave was six-feet tall. So even though he had to stoop to be within reach of his target, he had ample distance with which to build up momentum.

Edge fought in inner battle to rid his frame of tension. He had been hit hard many times. He knew there was less chance of a broken bone if a man was in a relaxed attitude at the time of impact. It was a hard struggle, because the fear of death was transmitted from his mind to every nerve ending in his body.

They did not want to kill him. He had believed that from the moment he saw who was holding up the stage. Four hardened cowpunchers were determined to make him pay for humiliating them at the way station. Two of them were much more eager to have revenge than the other two. All four were stone cold sober and the differences between them were more clearly seen than when they were drunk.

Ward and Sonny, standing on the rock on the other side of the Concord, were as frightened as the crew and passengers aboard the stagecoach about the outcome of what they witnessed. Ward even gaped his mouth wide as if to scream a demand that it stop.

And maybe he did.

But Edge failed to hear it. At that instant the viciously swung barrel of Dave's Winchester slammed into him. His hearing was gone, his sight, too. Also his sense of smell and taste. He was left only with feeling. All he could feel was excruciating agony.

He knew the blow had not killed him. During a second of crystal clear thinking he experienced a massive surge of sweet relief—that his worst fear was not realized. Dave had not stoved in his skull with the rifle barrel. Instead, he had aimed directly downwards, to crash the Winchester against his right shoulder.

Agony exploded from the point of impact to send searingly hot bolts through every fiber of his being.

He did not know if he screamed.

He was not aware of falling. First, he dropped hard to his knees, then pitched forward on to his belly, chest and face. Unable to soften this series of fresh blows against his flesh with his hands for the agony acted to paralyze him and his arms hung limply at his sides.

He was oblivious of the vomit that erupted from his stomach and spewed out of his mouth as he fell forward. He did not smell the stench of it nor felt the wetness as his face splashed into the pool it formed on the trail.

He failed to hear the booted feet thud against the ground to either side of him when Clyde and Dave leapt down from the rock. He did not feel one of Dave's feet hook under his belly, nor had any sensation of movement as he was rolled on his back.

125

"Get over here, you two!"

"What about these others?" Ward replied anxiously to Clyde's order.

"They ain't gonna do nothin'! On account he ain't nothin' to them!"

Ward and Sonny came down from their rock and circled around the front of the stalled stagecoach with their rifle barrels wavering as they continued to keep nervous watch on the driver and shotgun who still had their hands held high above their heads.

Charlie spat more tobacco juice between the rumps of the horses. "Beatin' up on him is okay, you boys," he growled. "But if it goes beyond that, you'll have to kill me as well as him."

He lowered his hands and looked intently at Harry Dodds. Who swallowed hard before he aped the other man's actions. Then he said huskily, "I'm with Charlie. Won't go for the piece in my holster or the rifle under my feet. Long as you don't stop that guy from breathin'."

"You got yourselves a deal," Clyde snapped as Ward and Sonny reached his side of the stagecoach. "Get the son of a bitch on his feet and up against the rock."

His eyes, glowing with the pleasure of anticipation, shifted quickly between Dave and Ward. Dave was fast dropping to his haunches and gripping the armpit under Edge's punished shoulder. Ward and Sonny eyed each other. Ward shook his head and Sonny stooped to hook a hand under the other armpit of the pain paralyzed man.

"Come on, damnit!" Clyde growled.

"Yeah, get it over with," Ward urged, turning his back on his three buddies. To face the stagecoach but with the Winchester angled across his chest.

Edge was aware of what was happening to him again. His shoulder felt as if there were a red hot poker sunk deep into it and his brain seemed numbed. He experienced only slight discomfort as he was dragged around in a half circle and then toward the rock from which the attack had been launched. He saw the two men who were dragging him and the one who followed in the tracks left by his boot heels. He saw the stagecoach.

Darkness had come rushing in across the desert and he could see nothing clearly. Not because of the poor light, though, but because his vision was blurred.

He could hear voices, but his hearing was still impaired. Sounds were merely scratches on his eardrums.

His viewpoint abruptly changed He was no longer on his back, being dragged over hard ground. He was up on his feet, but he was not supporting himself. His back was pressed against something harder and he was no longer moving.

He smelled his own vomit smeared across the bristles on his jaw. This threatened to erupt more from his belly. His eyes stung and he realized this was due to the saltiness of tears.

He heard clearly.

". . . gonna teach you a friggin' lesson, you son of a bitch! So you'll know if you ever run into us again, you won't be ready to poke your nose in where it ain't got no business."

"That's it, Clyde old buddy!" Dave squealed in excitement. "Make it so he don't have no nose!"

Edge felt like he was trapped in a waking

nightmare in which crazy things assumed vital importance. He could not be bothered to cling to fuzzy memories of what had happened to him, why it had happened, or who was responsible for his suffering. All that mattered was that he held his head high. This was necessary because if he were able to achieve this, then the rest of the muscles in his punished body might be encouraged to start working.

He hated to be helpless, having to rely on the men flanking him to keep him from slipping down the rock into an untidy heap at its base. It was just not in his nature to need help. Help was a favor and favors had to be returned.

With an enormous effort followed by a great sense of attainment, he forced his chin from his chest. A grin of pure pleasure took command of his face and ejected warmth into the ice blue slits of his eyes. He blinked once and teardrops were flicked off his eyelids.

He saw everything with perfect clarity in the dim, cool light of evening. And the nightmarish quality of what was happening to him was abruptly dispelled.

He saw Clyde in a half crouch in front of him poised to deliver a punch. His capacity to experience hatred spread out from his mind and filled his whole being the way the agony of the incapacitating blow had reached to the very limits of his sensory existence.

The new blow was launched at him. Clyde vented a shrill cry of triumph as his fist smashed into Edge's belly.

Edge hated the man who hurt him, but there was a bottomless reserve of the emotion to be directed at everyone and everything else in the world, past, present, and future.

The muscles of his legs and his arms refused to imitate those of his neck. So he was at the mercy of his attacker and the two men who flanked him. There was a burst of pain in his belly and at the small of his back as the force of the blow slammed him against the unmoving rock. Air rushed from his lungs and burst from his mouth. Bile tainted saliva spilled from his lips as his chin crashed down on to his chest again. His body sagged and he felt like his arms were to be jerked from their sockets as Dave and Sonny forced him to remain upright.

"That's wiped the friggin' smile off your friggin' face!" Clyde shrieked as he came erect, stepped closer to Edge and dragged the hat off his head. They grabbed a bunch of the jet black hair at the crown and jerked upwards.

With his free hand he began to slap the lean, bristled, sickness and saliva run face with the palm and then the back of the knuckles. He slammed hard enough to knock the head from side to side within the limits imposed by the hand grasping the hair.

He spoke with a vicious, rasping sound as he delivered the regular slaps.

"Findin' out what it's like to be on the receivin' end now, ain't you, mister? Gettin' shown up real good in front of folks. You ain't so friggin' tough, you stinkin' bounty hunter. Not without some skinny, titless woman to back you with the gun. We're givin' the orders now. And we're givin' them to a lousy Mex greaser who ain't in no position to argue."

He gave up on the slapping and folded the punishing hand into a fist again. He began to land short, jabbing punches against Edge's nose.

This hurt more than the slapping and soon produced a trickle of blood that developed into a steady flow, running from both nostrils and into the open mouth of the helpless man. The warmth and saltiness of the liquid on his tongue threatened to erupt more vomit from deep inside him.

Edge was too engulfed by the depthless ocean of hatred to be aware of this. He could hear what was being said to him. He was able to see everything that was directly in front of him. He felt each blow that landed against him.

Each and every part of what he heard, saw, and felt provided fresh fuel for the hatred that somehow acted to insulate him from the full force of his punishment.

Clyde, Dave, Sonny, and Ward were all going to die. Also Joe Straw, who he would take to Crater and hand over to be hanged without further consideration of why the half-breed Comanche had been driven to do what he did.

Charlie and Harry Dodds were objects of hatred as they sat up on the high seat of the Concord, looking down at him with pity on their time-lined faces. Likewise Mrs. Dora Naulty who peered out through the open doorway of the stagecoach, expressing grimacing shock. Tait and Carver kept their eyes averted from the scene of the beating.

All of them in some way or other had contributed to circumstances which led to Edge taking this punishment. These people and many like

130

them entered his life, and by the mundane ordinariness of what they were, caused him to question what he was.

Shit, he was what he had become. He was not like anybody else in the entire world. So what if he did not enjoy the pleasures that gave others happiness? He had what very few others possessed. He had freedom.

Not right at this very moment, that was sure. Pinned to a rock by two men while a third beat up on him. But this was a temporary state. When the grudge carrying cowpunchers had satiated their lust for revenge, they would leave him unconscious to wake up to agony. Perhaps they would stop short of the point where merciful oblivion closed in on him, not allowing his body to recover by one degree while he was unable to experience the suffering.

When they left him, they would still be prisoners of their instincts and emotions which ruled their actions and reactions. They were four young cowpunchers between jobs, hopes, dreams, desires, and ambitions. They were caught in a trap because their lives had a direction and to maintain it they had to abide by certain conventions imposed by society.

Edge's chin was back down on his chest. Clyde was using both hands clenched into fists now to smash punches against the belly of the trapped man.

Soon it would be over and Edge would be free again. He would not die. Even if Clyde was so filled with hatred he was incapable of realizing when the brutal punishment he was delivering reached the point where another blow would kill his victim, his buddies would intervene—Ward, Sonny, or even Dave, objectively on the fringe of the vicious beating. They were able to apply rational thinking to the consequences if Clyde should beat this man to death, how society would react, and to enforce changes of directions. Guilt—their own and their friend's—would punish and alter them.

Edge was close to unconsciousness. People were shouting close by, but the words seemed to be travelling over vast distances before they reached him. The sound of the voices was fuzzy in the same way as the blows against his belly were discernible as no more than dull thuds, blessedly painless.

"That's enough, Clyde!"

"It sure is, for you! Here, you hold the bastard while I take a turn!"

"I don't figure he can take any more, Dave!"

"Stay awake, you bastard! Don't you friggin' black out on me!"

Then Mrs. Dora Naulty said, "Stop it! You men, do something! If they don't kill him, they'll maim him for life!"

Edge experienced a surge of exhilaration which had nothing to do with the sudden inability to experience pain. The majority opinion was in favor of bringing the beating to an end.

He was no longer a prisoner of convention and his own emotions. In truth, he never had been—not since he shrugged out of the identity of Josiah C. Hedges and became the man called Edge.

He had not loved Crystal Dickens nor Beth. He did not envy the pathetic desires of Joe Straw, the do-gooder old lady, the other passengers, the driver, and shotgun aboard the stagecoach, the kid cowpunches, the Fords, the Hackmans, nor everyone else who had crossed his path on the endless trail he rode.

It was Josiah C. Hedges who harbored these feelings and he was dead. He existed as no more than a ghostly memory in the darkest recesses of the Edge's mind.

How many times had he emerged from the depths to influence the thinking and actions of Edge? A lot, that was sure. Every time he did it resulted in anguish or agony to punish the mind or body of the shell that hosted his spirit.

But no more. Never again would he be allowed to occupy the host mind or dictate the responses of the physical being he had once possessed, to introduce an identity crisis and leave the man called Edge open to attack while he struggled against an ethereal enemy who he thought was laid to rest long ago.

It had taken him many years to rid himself of the conviction that his life was ruled by cruel fates intent upon causing him suffering for past sins. A sense of triumph had swamped him then, but the elation he felt then was nothing to the soaring joy that filled him now. It formed an impenetrable barrier against the pain, humiliation, anger, and hatred that the beating had earlier generated.

His physical condition could not have been further removed from the state of his mind. The extent of his punishment was seen when Ward whirled toward Clyde and dragged him out of reach of the man held to the rock. Ward had to discard his rifle and lock both arms around the

133

waist of his friend to pull him clear. While this took place, Sonny released his hold on Edge. Dave cursed as loudly and shrilly as Clyde. As Clyde was unable to break free of Ward's grip on him, Dave could not keep the two hundred pounds weight of Edge upright. Edge fell forward with a twisting action. Dave had to let go of him and the shoulder of the almost unconscious man hit the ground. His arm swung through the air and acted to shift his center of gravity. Although he landed on his side, he was moved to an involuntary half roll and came to rest on his back, one arm held beneath him, one flung to the side, and both legs splayed, his face exposed to the glittering light of the newly risen moon.

"Dear God in Heaven, what have you done to him?" the old woman screamed. "You've killed him!"

She rose from her seat and half fell as she struggled from the stagecoach.

"No they ain't," Harry Dodds argued. "He's still breathin'!"

Charlie spat tobacco juice and growled, "That's good, partner. Means we don't have to take no hand in this."

Clyde had ceased trying to tear himself away from Ward, who released him. Sonny stepped to the side, from between Dave and the sprawled form of Edge.

All four cowpunchers gazed silently down at their victim.

His mouth was hanging open to give access and exit to air which was unable to force a way through the crusted blood blocking his nostrils. There was more congealed blood on his lips and teeth and among the stubble of his day-old beard. His nose was no longer angular and the lean look had gone out of his cheeks. For the beating had swollen his flesh with dark colored contusions. Sweat and vomit was smeared on every part of his face.

Ward and Sonny looked close to throwing up themselves. Dave showed a grimace of frustration. Clyde, drained by anger and exertion, forced a grin across his face.

"I sure as hell give it to him, didn't I, old buddies?"

"You sure as hell didn't give the rest of us a chance, frig it!" Dave snarled.

"You are wicked, evil boys!" Mrs. Naulty accused, and she advanced to Edge. She was brought to a halt and rooted to the spot when Dave whirled toward her and ordered, "Stay outta this, you old crow! I gotta powerful urge to hit somebody!"

He fisted one hand and cracked it into the palm of the other.

"Now, son, there's no call to go insultin' a lady that way," Charlie muttered nervously.

Dave wrenched his head around to turn his glowering eyes toward the bearded driver.

"Clyde!" Ward yelled. "I think it's time we left!"

"Yeah!" Sonny agreed. "We done what we wanted."

Clyde ended his gloating, curtailed the grin and looked around at his friends and the tense witnesses to see what had happened.

He nodded, "That's right, old buddies." Now he showed a personable smile to the old lady and the men aboard the Concord. "Like to thank you

135

people for not interferin'. We said we didn't wanna kill nobody, and we didn't. Paid a debt is all."

He stooped to retrieve his discarded Winchester and his friends followed his example. Ward and Sonny eagerly, Dave with embittered reluctance.

"Okay, lady," Clyde told Mrs. Naulty. "You wanna take care of the Mex, you can do it now."

The woman came slowly to Edge, casting apprehensive glances at the glowering Dave. The man done out of his fair share of vengeance responded to the jerk of Clyde's head and followed Ward and Sonny. Clyde brought up the rear of the line that went across the trail between the stalled stagecoach and the dead mule, then he went out of sight into the rocks toward the place where their horses were tethered.

Edge had never lost consciousness. He came close when the short-lived elation left him and the barrier against pain was lifted. He was assaulted by waves of agony from every part of his body, the most hard to bear source being concentrated at his belly. When this hit him, there was an almost overwhelming desire to jerk up his legs, roll on to his side, and fold himself double in the hope such actions would ease the pain.

This would have betrayed the false impression of unconsciousness—maybe invited an instinctive assault from Dave, more brutal punches, a vicious kick, or even a gunshot. He could take no further punishment and remain awake, but by enduring the effects of existing pain to prevent being subjected to a second beating, he came within a heartbeat of defeating his aim. The effort required to suffer without any attempt to gain ease drained him of all but the final iota of willpower that kept him from sinking into oblivion.

Nobody saw the fresh beads of sweat that oozed from his pores while he was engaged in this inner combat nor heard the soft sigh that emerged between his bloodstained teeth when he won the fight to cling on to awareness.

He heard Clyde speak to Mrs. Dora Naulty and then the footfalls of the four cowpunchers as they moved away from him. He waited until Charlie spat and Harry Dodds growled, "I gotta take a leak, Charlie. I ain't never been so scared in my life before."

The sounds he made climbing down from the Concord masked the footfalls of the men heading for their horses.

The woman kneeling beside Edge took a sharp intake of breath when she saw his lids crack open and the slivers of his eyes glinting in the moonlight.

"Don't move, young man," she said in a soft, rasping tone.

Edge did draw up his legs and roll on to his side, but not to ease his pain, but simply because it provided the only series of actions by which he could rise to his feet. He was uncaring that his movements caused him to collide with the kneeling woman and sent her toppling to the ground with a choked cry of alarm.

Edge was totally ignorant of her proximity. He did not know that the small sound she made had drawn every pair of eyes to stare at him.

Harry Dodds was behind a rock, his head wrenched around as he relieved himself.

137

Charlie, tobacco juice running down his chin, sat transfixed on the high seat of the Concord.

Tait and Carver, rooted to where they stood, flanked the open door of the stagecoach from which they had climbed down.

Only Joe Straw did not gaze with shocked incredulity at Edge and remained in the same posture of feigned drunken sleep that he had held since he first recovered from the stupor—an hour before the stagecoach was forced to halt, waiting for an opportunity to escape the man who was taking him to face the hanging rope.

Edge was unable to unfold completely upright, the fire in his belly forcing him to remain in a half stoop as he made a complete turn to get his bearings. He saw his revolver first, lying on the trail, its oiled surface gleaming softly in the moonlight. He ignored this and finally saw the Concord—with the Winchester leaning against the rear wheel.

He almost toppled to the ground when he made the shuffling turn, which warned him to be wary of falling as he took short, painful steps toward his objective. He clutched at his belly with both hands and rocked from side to side at each pace.

"What you going to do?" the woman rasped as she made it onto her hands and knees.

"Whatever, he sure as hell ain't gonna let anyone stop him doin' it, lady," Charlie growled.

Tait and Carver stumbled in their hurry to get away from the side of the stagecoach.

Despite the bruised and smeared condition of his face, it was impossible not to see the depth of hatred transcending pain that was expressed upon it.

The teeth were clenched together and a grunt

138

of triumph hissed through them as one hand came away from his belly and fisted around the night-cooled barrel of the Winchester.

He rested for a second, his hate-filled eyes fastened upon the slumped form of Joe Straw.

The half-breed Comanche heard his labored breathing and sensed the degree of powerful emotion that was keeping Edge on his feet. For that fleeting time while the man was little more than the thickness of a window pane from him, Straw was in the grip of terror. He was certain to be blamed for what had happened.

Edge turned and moved painfully but relentlessly away. The cold air dried the sweat of fear that covered Straw from head to toe.

Dodds was out from behind the rock and the woman was on her feet again. They remained as still as Charlie, Tait, and Carver. Everyone stared at Edge certain that with every dragging step he took that he would slump to the ground.

But he did not. He made it along the side of the Concord and then to the front of the team. He came to a halt, between the two lead horses and the dead mule. When all the watchers held their breath—sure the final step had drained him and they were about to see him pitch unconscious across the carcass.

But this, too, was not to be.

He turned, legs splayed so that this feet were placed a little wider than his shoulders, facing out along the trail that cut across the spartanly featured desert. The rifle, which he had dragged wearily behind him, was raised and held in a double-handed grip across the base of his belly,

He did not straighten up.

"Charlie, he's gonna—" Dodds started.

"What he ain't gonna do is get me killed!" the driver cut in, the forcefully spoken words ejecting the wad of tobacco from his mouth. He scrambled to get down off the high seat of the Concord.

When he was in the position he had struggled to hard to attain, Edge squeezed his eyes tightly closed. He concentrated his entire being on summoning the strength to straighten up. He could not prevent a grunt from escaping his throat.

He clearly heard the exchange between the driver and shotgun. For the first time in a long while, he tasted blood in his mouth.

Fresh fires roared in his left shoulder and at the pit of his stomach. His head felt twice the normal size. For long moments he was unaware of anything outside of his own agony. He knew he did not dare to open his eyes yet, that nothing he saw would be in focus and this would threaten his sense of balance. If he fell, he would be finished.

He smelled his vomit, then the stink of the dead mule.

He heard one of the team horses snort, then the beat of hooves from further away.

Bile negated the taste of blood in his mouth.

He became aware of the grease of sweat on his hands fisted around the barrel and frame of the Winchester.

Hatred began a fresh attack on pain.

He opened his eyes and blinked once to rid the lashes of sweat. He was gripped by the sensation that never before had he been able to see so clearly at night.

The hoofbeats rose to the cadence of a gallop, but the sound was receding. The blood caked along his top lip cracked as he formed his mouth into the line of a grimace.

He turned his head slightly to the left and saw with perfect definition the jagged line which the last of the scattering rocks inscribed against the background of the desert.

When he raised the rifle to nestle the stock against his left shoulder, a bone in his right one made a clicking sound that triggered the most powerful bolt of pain yet.

He thumbed back the hammer as he rested his cheek against the cool wood of the stock. His vision blurred once more and he experienced a split second of despair that he no longer had the willpower to resist the demands of agony.

Then Mrs. Dora Naulty shrieked, "They'll kill you, you fool!"

She was a closer target of hate. The rock still, glowering, unbreathing, and unblinking Edge abruptly felt physically weighed down with venomous malevolence for her. He might well have whirled and blasted every bullet in the rifle at her had not the four men ridden into his sight from beyond the rocks. His hatred was immediately transferred to those who had earned it.

All sensation of pain was gone and he was seeing clearly again—over a range of some three hundred yards.

He triggered a shot.

Behind him, Tait, Carver, and Charlie threw themselves to the ground while Harry Dodds ran to Mrs. Naulty and curled an arm around her thin waist so that they went down together.

Joe Straw hunched lower in his seat and raised his hands. He began to gnaw at the twine which bound his wrists. His head felt leaden and ached from the liquor and the long sleep.

Sonny threw his arms in the air and pitched sideways from his saddle, a bloodstain blossoming on his chest.

The cry that was vented by Edge was partly of triumph, partly of pain. It lengthened and was entirely powered by pain as he pumped the lever action of the Winchester.

The riders had been angling out of the rocks to get on the trail, glancing back at the stalled stagecoach. But none of them saw the man with the levelled rifle in front of the head of the team until the sound of the shot cracked against the thud of galloping hooves.

There was a moment of shock as they saw one of their number fall.

The animalistic sound venting from the throat of Edge took on the tone of a battlecry as he squeezed the trigger again. He saw with perfect clarity in the bright moonlight the splash of dark blood that arched away from the head of Dave.

The cowpuncher tried desperately to cling to his saddlehorn but the strength drained from him and he tumbled through the dust raised by the galloping horses.

Edge was like a machine in the precise way in which he jacked a fresh shell into the breech as the empty case was ejected. While the constant pitch sound shrieking from his mouth could have been some alarm device to warn that the mechanism was nearing the overload breaking point.

Clyde and Ward wheeled to the left—intent upon a turn and race for the cover of the rocks.

A third shot took Clyde in the back, sent him

142

crashing into the neck of his mount. Then he bounced off and did a half corkscrew turn over the rear of the horse.

The expended portion of the bullet that killed him hit the ground before he did and the rifle had been tracked to the side to draw a bead on Ward, who had completed the turn and was frantically drawing his rifle from the boot a few yards from gaining the safety of the rocks.

A fourth shot and another hit, the bullet drilling into the side of the man's neck. The rifle he had drawn was sent sailing through the air and the cowpuncher went off the side of his mount. One foot was trapped in a stirrup and the horse veered off course trying to get free of the drag needed to run several yards before he succeeded.

Edge had emptied the Winchester. In a rhythmic series of actions, he jacked bullets into the breech and squeezed the trigger to blast them from the muzzle. He tracked the barrel to left and right, and aimed at the sprawled bodies clearly visible now that the dust of pumping hooves had settled. He saw the twitch of movement as each bullet drilled into unfeeling flesh.

He drew no distinction between the four young men. It did not matter who had beaten him, held him, called him a Mex and a greaser, or aimed a gun at him. They were four, but they were one, each sharing in the responsibility of what the others did. And what they did to one man . . . a man who had finally figured out that he could be but one man . . .

The battlecry had become a gasping sound now.

The firing pin fell into an empty breech with a dry click.

The beat of hooves faded as the riderless horses raced into the distance.

Edge was unaware that the empty rifle had fallen from his hands. He did know that the night could not, in reality, have darkened to an inky blackness so quickly.

With the prime objects of his all-consuming hatred having spilled their lifeblood on the arid desert, he had nothing left with which he could combat the torrent of pain that was abruptly undamned. He gaped his mouth wide to give vent to a vocal response, but no sound emerged. He dropped hard to his knees and it was as if the impact detonated a bolt of iron that blasted up through his body to explode against the inside of his skull. He toppled forward and sprawled across the long dead carcass of the hapless mule, the putrefying flesh of the animal breaking his fall which he did not feel.

Charlie came to him first. Then Tait, followed by Carver. Finally, Harry Dodds, came, who needed to support Mrs. Dora Naulty with a hand cupped under one of her elbows.

While they were forming an archlike line around the unconscious man, Joe Straw eased himself out of the Concord with his hands still tightly bound at the wrists. He was still drunk and he cursed silently at the effort required to keep from staggering. He managed to untie the reins of the gelding from the rear of the stage coach.

"Did you ever see anythin' like that in your life before, Charlie?" Dodds asked huskily.

The bearded old timer bit off a chew of tobacco and extracted some juice from it before he answered, "Never did, Harry. Reckon it's what they call mind over matter. He ought never have been able to get on his feet. Let alone walk over here and shoot down them four guys easy as apples in a barrel."

Joe Straw climbed up onto the rear wheel of the Concord and tugged on the reins to bring the gelding level with him. Nobody who stood surveying the man sprawled across the mule paid any attention to the clop of hooves as the horse moved into the required position.

They did whirl around when Straw slammed astride the animal's back and lunged him into a gallop with a yell and a thud of spurred heels.

"Because of the son of a bitch is as muleheaded as that animal he fell on!" the half-breed Comanche shrieked as he raced his mount around the group of shocked people and out onto the trail beyond, clinging to both the reins and the gelding's mane with his bound hands.

Dodds instinctively reached for his holstered revolver. He looked relieved when his partner shot forward a hand to check the move.

"This guy seems to have what's needed to take care of his own problems, Harry," the bearded old timer growled.

Franklin Carver had to clear his throat before he could speak. "He's not going to be very pleased when he wakes up and discovers we allowed his prisoner to escape, wouldn't you say?"

They all stared out along the trail to where Joe Straw was still holding the gelding to a high speed gallop.

"Perhaps we should be far away from here when he does wake up," Dwight Tait suggested.

"No, I will not allow you to abandon him out here in the wilderness!" the woman snapped.

"I ain't gonna, Mrs. Naulty," Charlie said sourly.

"It's pleasing to know one of you men has the milk of human kindness running through him," she hissed, with a look of contempt shared equally among Carver, Tait and Dodds, from whom she stepped away with a wrench of her arm.

Charlie spat and shook his head. "Just blood. And after I just seen what he's capable of when he oughta be kickin' around in the dust and screamin', I'd hate to have him lookin' for me to spill it when he's fit and well."

Carver swallowed hard. "Makes sense, Dwight."

Dodds nodded his agreement.

"So all right," the driver muttered grimly. "You two fellers get him aboard the stagecoach while Harry and me use his horse to drag the mule outta our way. We should reach Way Station Number Two in a couple of hours and if he's still out, we can leave him there." He looked straight at the woman. "And this time, we ain't gonna bury his dead."

"If you won't, you won't. But while you attend to what must be done, I will pray for their departed souls. They were some mothers's sons."

She went to the side of the trail, faced out to where the four dead men were humped on the desert, clasped her hands under her chin and bowed her head.

Carver dropped to his haunches beside Edge

146

and muttered with admiration, "He's some kind of tough egg, wouldn't you say, Dwight?"

The aged driver and shotgun moved toward the mare tied to the rear of the stage.

"Hard-boiled as they come," Tait said as he stooped to take a grip on the shoulders of the prone man. He could not suppress a shrill and nervous giggle.

"What's so funny, Dwight?" his partner wanted to know with a start.

"Egg, Franklin. Hard-boiled most of the time, there's no doubt." He gently raised one shoulder of the unconscious man as Carver gripped the ankles. "But in the event he happens to wake up right at this moment, we better see that for him it's over easy."

Chapter Eleven

Edge did not wake up until sunrise the next morning and for several seconds after he cracked open his eyes at the insistence of the bright yellow light he was totally disorientated.

He knew that he was in a bed in a small room with a window that faced east. He also knew that he was naked under the covers and that his head felt fuzzy, as after a long drinking jag followed by a much longer period of drunken sleep.

He attempted to sit up against the headboard so that he could see more than the sun bright ceiling of the room. The pain hit him, exploded white heat in his belly, his right shoulder, and in every part of his head. He gagged but only air wretched up from his stomach to rattle in his parched throat.

He lay still, waiting for the sharpness of the agony to become dulled. He had total recall of every event from the moment he first saw Joe Straw until he exploded the final shot from his Winchester on that brightly moonlit night when four cowpunchers paid the ultimate price for tangling with the man called Edge.

He grinned, uncaring that the expression caused the skin of his lower face to smart. He felt no sympathy for the quartet of young men who had no way of knowing what kind of trouble they were messing in when stopped that stage. Irrespective of that, by their actions they had taught Edge what kind of a man he was.

It was very quiet in the room and outside. During the more than thirty minutes it took him to sit up, ease out of bed, and get to his feet, he heard only his labored breathing and the creak of bedsprings. Without hatred to combat pain, he had only strong determination to keep him from surrendering to the physical and mental demands for a much longer period of rest.

His clothing was draped over a chair beside the bed and it took him thirty minutes to dress. Everything was stiff with stale sweat and the shirt smelled of vomit.

He had to go to the other side of the bed to get to the bureau with a mirror upon it and a water pitcher in a bowl. His Winchester leaned against the front of the bureau. His revolver and the razor lay on top of it. He pushed the revolver into the holster after checking it was fully loaded. Then he stowed the razor in the neck pouch.

Only then did he look at his reflection in the cracked mirror.

The blood and vomit had been cleaned from his face, along with the sweat and the trail dust. He saw that his nose was swollen and blotched with dull colors. Likewise his cheeks, but the purple and black areas here were camouflaged by the thick growth of black bristles long enough to show it was the morning after the night of the beating.

He regarded his reflecton for a few moments, and showed another grin as he rasped softly, "Damn shame I never got to see the other fellers." He became impassive and icy-eyed to ask his image, "Where's Joe Straw?"

Then he picked up the Winchester and knew from its weight that it was empty. He carried it at his side as he went to a closet door and pulled it open. Inside there was dust and a rail from which clothes hangers hung. He found it less painful to hoist the mattress and look down through the springs rather than to drop to his haunches to check beneath the bed. More dust was all, the same as in the three drawers of the bureau.

So his gear, including a saddlebag with close to three thousand dollars in it, was not in the room.

He elected to go to the window before trying the door, and he discovered he was in a second-story room of a building on a curve of the trail. It was situated directly on the side of the trail that curved at this point to sweep around the base of a hill above the point where the sun was poised.

When Edge looked to his right he saw that the trail straightened from the bend to head in a direct line across the scrub desert to the south. Because the morning was newly born and there was not yet a shimmering heat haze to advance the horizon, he was able to see the ridges, dark and jagged, of the Santa Rosa Mountains that showed above the curvature of the earth.

Way Station Number Three was not in sight, but hidden in some shallow hollow or behind a low rise. Likewise the rocky area where the stage-coach had been ambushed.

Not that it mattered. The southern section of the trail and all that had happened along it was behind Edge, another series of violent events in his past.

His eyes cracked to glinting slits against the brightness of the sun, and he swept his gaze in from the desert, over the rocky slope of the hill and out along the trail that cut through other hills to mark the way north. These rises would be the Momoli Mountains, he knew.

He did not know any town, in this part of the territory and from his restricted viewpoint at the window, which did not open, he could see no other buildings. So another way station, he guessed, basking silently in the early morning sunlight. Providing facilities and accommodation for stagecoach passengers to rest for the night. In this instance before the elderly Charlie and Harry called stagetime to the motley group of passengers and they boarded to head out along the trail that snaked away on a slight upgrade through the Momoli Mountains somewhere to the north of which lay Phoenix.

Edge rolled a cigarette as he surveyed the peaceful scene beyond the window. Then he lit it and drew his lungs full of smoke. Every move he made was painful—even when he altered his expression—but he experienced a keen sense of satisfaction. His physical injuries would heal. Of far greater importance to him was that never again would he allow himself to suffer from the more debilitating hurt of mental anguish.

He finished smoking the cigarette and crushed

it out against the window pane. He dropped the mangled remains to the floor and experienced the first nagging doubt about his present circumstances.

The sun was well clear of the hilltop across the trail, and hot enough to form an arc of shimmering haze out on the desert. Yet still the building was locked in silence.

Even if the people off the stagecoach were deeply asleep, recovering from the long day's trip and the shock of the violence at the ambush, surely whoever ran the way station should have begun the routine chores by now.

Then he did hear a sound. It took several seconds to identify it as a grunt vented from his own lips. Sweat oozed from every pore, greasing his hands and face and pasting his clothes to his body, but the brief period of tension was gone. It was just pain and the heat that beaded the sweat from his flesh for he was thinking clearly. Somebody had taken care of him. His guns had been left in the room, which had to mean the door would be unlocked. So he was not a captive and there was no intention to harm him.

Then he heard something else, but he did not utter a sound. It did not originate within the building.

It came through the hills from the north.

A shout.

He pushed the side of his face close to the windowpane to widen his angle of vision in that direction so that he was able to see the entire length of the trail until it twisted out of sight between the fold of two hills.

There was a gunshot and then the thunder of

galloping hooves, the rattle of spinning wheels. All of this was muted by distance and the intervening high ground.

Then a stagecoach plunged into view. It was the better part of a mile away. The Concord and its four-horse team was plain to see for a moment, then it was enveloped in the billowing cloud of dust raised by the pumping hooves of the straining horses and the sliding wheels as they came too fast around the curve out of the twin hills.

For a few more seconds the Concord was in danger of listing too far to the side and toppling over off the side of the trail. But then it rocked in the opposite direction a moment before two wheels were about to be lifted off the ground.

Edge could see the two sweat-lathered lead horses of the team clearly now. He caught brief glimpses of the other two and the Concord as it rolled and pitched for many headlong yards before straightening.

Men were yelling within the building. Edge wrenched his intrigued gaze away from the dust shrouded stagecoach to look down at the trail immediately below the window.

A door was wrenched open and the two men ran through it. Both were clad in nightshirts. One was about fifty, six-feet tall and very thin, almost bald, with sunken eyes and very little chin. The other was more a boy than a man. He was no more than eighteen, blond and a head shorter than the man who was undoubtedly his father—this seen in the way his mouth was also so close to the point of his jaw.

They continued to shout at each other as they fisted the grit of sleep from their eyes, but what they said could not be heard against the cacophony of sound made by the racing stage.

The dust cloud was now elongated, stretched out behind the Concord. Edge, back from the window, was able to recognize Charlie and Harry up on the box seat as he switched his gaze away from the father and son who had just awakened.

Again he was allowed a mere glimpse before lots of dust flung upwards to totally engulf the team and the Concord. This was caused by the locked rear wheels of the stagecoach which ceased to turn and now slithered along the trail as the brake blocks grabbed at the rims, and the abrupt change of pace of the four horses when they responded to the driver's demand for a halt.

For the time that it took for the team and their burden to come to a frenetic stop immediately below the window, Edge needed to make a conscious effort to convince himself he was awake and that he was not experiencing some vivid fantasy conjured up by his disorientated mind while his body was still recovering from the effects of the beating.

He did this by concentrating on the pain that wracked him from head to toe. Sleep, of which dreams and nightmares were a part, blotted out pain. If he was hurting this much, he had to be awake.

Yet something he had seen through the window gave the scene in front of the building the quality of the unreal, something his narrowed eyes had witnessed for part of a second before the billowing dust veiled it.

Now the dust began to settle and there was a moment of silence.

The team of horses snorted their exhaustion.

The man and the boy shouted in unison. The tone of their voices was questioning but the force of each word cancelled the sense of what it competed with.

The ropes! Edge's mind filled with the memory of what he had seen during that instant of clear vision. It was Joe Straw who was scheduled to be hanged. Yet Harry Dodds and Charlie had ropes tied around their necks.

Gunfire exploded and the shouting voices were curtailed.

If there were screams, the din of the rifle shots masked them. Probably there were none. The father and son must have died instantly, at least one of the bullets tearing into their flesh striking deep into a vital organ. They were hit where they stood with no opportunity to turn and run for the cover of the building when they saw the danger. They crumpled to the ground, the gray fabric of their nightshirts blossoming with bloodstains, separate for a moment, then merged into one great dark area.

Edge instinctively reached for his holstered Colt and released his hold on the empty Winchester as he folded to the wall beside the window.

The shooting ended and when he peered out from one side of the window he ignored the inert, bullet riddled corpses to survey the ancient Concord, and the men who were climbing from it, their repeater rifles covering the dead and the facade of the building.

There were six of them, five coming through the door of the stage and one from the roof. There were five Indians and one half Indian, all with Comanche blood running through their veins.

"What did I tell you, man?" Joe Straw yelled as he hit the ground after jumping the final three feet from the roof. "Didn't I tell you it'd be a piece of cake? Easy as friggin' pie!"

He was in a state of high excitement which did not infect the wretched looking full blood Comanches who seemed not to hear him as they kept cautious watch on the facade of the building, raking their suspicious eyes over the open doorway and the windows, blinking whenever they glanced at the panes of the upper story, dazzled by the sunlight striking the glass.

Then one of the braves growled, "We not want to hear talk of food, Joe Straw. We want to eat it."

"Then come and get it," the half-breed invited confidently, pushing between two of the tensely apprehensive Comanches to step around the bloodstained corpses and head for the doorway. "Weren't nobody here but these two."

One of the braves tracked his Winchester around to aim at the back of the swaggering Straw, but the obvious leader of the band put out a hand to direct the rifle muzzle down at the ground. He shook his head in mild rebuke, whispered a few words which drew a response of nods.

Then the leader aimed his own repeater straight at the sky and triggered three shots in quick succession. They all looked back along the north trail and within moments another Indian showed himself between the hills, riding a pony and leading a string of others roped together.

"Now, we eat," the Comanche announced as he

lowered his rifle and started for the doorway through which Joe Straw had gone.

Edge jutted out his lower lip and softly blew a draught of cool air over his bruised and sweat sheened features. Then he muttered, "Big order, but somehow I got to see you fellers have bit off more than you can chew."

Chapter Twelve

The elderly driver and shotgun had taken several bullets in their chests. They were held upright on the high seat by ropes encircling their waists and tied to the handrails at either side. This was in addition to the ropes Edge first saw—noosed around their necks and lashed to the rails of the baggage rack.

It was a ploy that would have fooled no one if the Concord had come into view at a sedate pace. But the billowing dust erupted by the headlong gallop had masked the limp postures and the restraining ropes. Likewise, Joe Straw stretched out full-length among the baggage, steering the team with reins that were lengthened with another piece of rope. The shattered windows and bullet pocked timbers of the stagecoach provided further evidence of a holdup of far greater violence than that undertaken by the grudge carrying cowpunchers.

Edge surveyed the stalled stagecoach only briefly and gave no consideration at all to the fates of Dora Naulty, Franklin Carver, and Dwight Tait. He watched the sixth Comanche bring the string of unshod ponies to the front of the building, dismount, and join the others inside without tethering the animals.

The ponies were as underfed, unhealthy, and sorry looking as their owners, but far less dangerous. As soon as the sixth Comanche was inside, Edge curtailed his disjointed thinking about how this threatening situation had come about to concentrate upon surviving it.

He could hear them downstairs, shouting and laughing, banging doors open and closed, and rattling pots and pans and breaking glass. Much of what was said was in the Comanche tongue, but Joe Straw often yelled loud enough to be heard above the general din, obsequiously boastful of how he was responsible for the good fortune.

"And ain't it like I said it would be . . . All this grub and liquor for the takin' . . . Ain't you glad you listened to me instead of . . . When we're through here, we can head down the trail . . . Pull the same trick at the next way station . . . But we gotta take care we don't kill the woman that's there . . . Anyway, not until after we . . ."

Edge moved painfully and silently from the window to the door, right hand draped over the butt of the holstered Colt and left fisted around the frame of the Winchester. He no longer concentrated upon picking out what Straw was yelling above the din. He was certain the half-breed Comanche did not know his former captor was in the building, which would have been very puzzling to Edge had he allowed his mind free rein to drift back into thoughts of what happened

160

between the time he slumped into unconsciousness and when he came out of it in this room.

What he did know for certain was that the hapless Joe Straw was as much a prisoner as he had been before Edge took the beating. He was in line to be killed as soon as it pleased the leader of the hungry, filthy, ill-clothed and murderous Comanches to give the order.

It was just as certain that Joe Straw knew this. His high excitement at the success of the attack on this way station had begun to ring more false with every shrill word he yelled. His attitude was at once a bravado attempt to convince himself that his suspicion was unfounded and a constant plea to convince the Comanches that he could continue to be useful to them with his actual terror discernible just beneath the paper thin surface of his desperate raucousness.

A man like Joe Straw was familiar with desperate situations. Had he known Edge was close at hand and chosen not to reveal this to the Comanches, he would have had the wits to signal by gesture or words that he knew.

Edge cracked open the door of the room and peered out across a small landing with the top of a narrow stairway directly opposite. He smelled smoke and during a momentary lull in vocal sounds from below heard the crackle of burning wood. He eased the door open wider and thrust his head out to look to the left and right.

He saw that the landing ran for the width of the building with several doors in the facing walls. The doors had numbers on them, which explained why he did not hear the father and son roused from sleep before they left the building.

161

The private quarters of the way station were downstairs.

He stepped out onto the landing, which had no windows except for the stained glass transoms above each door. He closed the door of the room in which he had rested and this diminished the level of light to a pleasant green hue as the harsh blaze of the sun was filtered through the colored transoms.

There was still a lot of loud noise downstairs, the Comanches continuing to revel in unaccustomed plenty. Joe Straw sought shrilly to impress upon the braves that it was all due to him, and their good fortune did not have to end at this way station.

"Look, man, we don't have to use the stage again! The guy and his wife who run the place down the trail know me! Guess they'll be real curious to see me ridin' up to the station, but they won't—"

The Comanches had stopped talking among themselves to listen to him and when he realized he had their full attention, Straw lowered his voice without allowing the tone of false enthusiasm to fade. The thud of a blow was muted, too. Perhaps by the man's red hair? He broke something made of glass as he fell, but the actual sound of his frame crashing to the floor was masked by a chorus of Comanche voices raised in delighted approval of what had happened.

Edge crossed the landing and entered a room of identical proportions, furnished in the same manner as the one he had just left. The view from the window however was over a fenced yard to a stable block built at the base of a fifty-feet high cliff. The empty corral was enclosed alongside of the stable, the yard, and the main building.

This window didn't open either. There was a fifteen foot drop to the dirt of the yard, which caused Edge to grimace at the mere fleeting thought of what fresh pains such a jump would erupt within his hurting body.

There was far less noise rising up the stairway now. The braves were eating and drinking and talking in normal conversational tones in their own tongue with just an occasional guffaw or thud of a fist on a table that rattled crockery. Edge trod carefully on the bare boarding as he moved to the end of the landing and was just as cautious in crossing another familiar looking room. This one was at the far end of the building from the room in which the Comanches were gathered at the rear of the building, at the angle formed by its corner and the fence that enclosed this side of the yard. Its window was non-opening.

He stood beside the window, waiting, sweating, and hurting, his mind devoid of thought, his bruised and bristled face expressionless.

He waited as long as ten minutes, during which the talk below became desultory and interrupted by several pauses of varying lengths. Then there was a curtailment rather than a fading away of what was being said, which was a signal that something was about to happen.

Edge turned sideways on to the window and raised his left arm, the elbow crooked.

Joe Straw screamed high, long lasting, animalistic sound that spoke volumes about the depth and breadth of the man's terror.

163

Edge crashed his elbow at the center of the window and could not withdraw it fast enough to prevent broken shards of glass from piercing his shirt sleeve and stabbing into his flesh.

Above the shrill scream, he heard the window-pane shatter at the blow, but not the crash of the glass against the dirt of the yard.

He waited a few seconds this time, his hearing strained to its limit as his right hand draped the jutting butt of the holstered Colt.

Then the scream subsided to a whimper.

"You say you are more Comanche than white eyes, Joe Straw! Comanche brave would not cry like baby because he is afraid!"

Triangular pieces of razor sharp glass were still held in the frame of the window. Edge began to ease them out very carefully, and set them down on the floor.

"What you gonna do to me?" Straw wailed.

"Kill you, Joe Straw."

"Nooooooo!"

The slap of a hand against bare flesh silenced the half-breed. An order was given in the Comanche language.

"Why? Why you doin' this to me after I—"

"You joined us to save your life, Joe Straw. And took a hand in killing the white-eyed blood brothers of your father. Are we to believe that you would not kill us—the blood brothers of your mother—if it suited your purpose?"

Edge had cleared enough glass from the base and sides of the frame to allow for his exit. He leaned far enough out to check that there was no rear window to the room in which Joe Straw was pleading a denial of what the leader of the

Comanches had said. Then he withdrew, went to the bed, and drew off its covers. He carried the mattress to the window. The tension that knotted his every muscle acted to sharpen the pain that assaulted him. He felt as if each bead of sweat oozing from his pores was a drop of strength draining from him.

"You got no reason to think that! I ain't never killed an Indian! But I killed plenty of whites! Whites, they all hate me for bein' part Comanche! But I ain't never been hated by no Indians for bein' what I am! Not until now! Oh, sweet Jesus, I'm startin' to burn!"

The mattress hit the ground with a dull thud. The empty Winchester fell on top of it with less noise.

"You want a cool drink, Joe Straw?"

A bottle was smashed and there was a strange roaring sound. Then another shrill scream vented by the half-breed. This time accompanied by a gust of cruel laughter.

Had Edge been curious about the reason for the series of sounds, he would not have been capable of rational thought. His mind was under attack by bolts of agony that felt as bad as any he experienced during the beating and its aftermath. He did not think he could survive the drop without passing out again.

He hung down the rear wall of the way station building, his fingertips curled over the ledge of the broken window, his boots dangling less than six feet above the mattress. It was a short enough drop under normal circumstances, but the act of climbing out the window and lowering himself gradually down the wall had stretched his punished flesh and the tissue and muscle beneath it. Both his shoulders and the lower area of his belly seemed to be at the seat of raging fires.

There was another scream.

He was certain it was vented involuntarily from his own throat and so it was an instinct for self-preservation that caused him to release his hold on the window ledge. His right hand streaked to the Colt and had it cocked and clear of the holster as he landed flat-footed on the mattress and fell to the side.

Tears filled his eyes and he squeezed the lids tightly closed. Nausea could erupt only bitter bile into his throat. One section of his mind longed for unconsciousness to flood through him and swamp the agony while another warned him this would be dangerous.

He was still screaming after an agonizing and agony-wracked time when his silence was of paramount importance. He dragged his free hand up to his mouth and discovered with exploring fingertips that his lips were curled back and his teeth were gritted. There was no rush of hot breath to power a scream.

The realization came that he was not venting a vocal response to suffering triggered rational thought from that part of his mind which had employed instinct to prevent the scream.

He opened his eyes, blinked away the stinging salt moisture of tears and sweat, and he stared at the weathered timber of the rear wall of the building. On the other side of the building, far down its length, Joe Straw ended his scream and begged, "Please. If I gotta die, make it quick. For God's sake, shoot me."

Edge heard his pent up breath whistle out between his clenched teeth. He rolled on to his belly and rose on all fours and fisted a hand around the frame of the empty Winchester before coming slowly up onto his knees. He needed the support of the wall to get to his feet.

Just as hatred had served to overcome the demands of pain for as long as it took to kill the men who beat him, anger acted to calm the waves of fresh agony that threatened to break over him and drown him into unconsciousness.

The Comanche bastards were killing Joe Straw. If Edge allowed them to do that, it had all been for nothing. Joe Straw had to be hanged by the people of Crater, Colorado—that was the deal—with a thousand dollar reward for the trouble Edge took.

"A blood brother of the Comanches would not beg for mercy, Joe Straw! Perhaps you would like another drink, eh? We have plenty to spare!"

More raucous approval was roared by the braves.

It had all been for nothing.

There was a door in the rear wall of the building and Edge staggered toward it.

Too many people had died.

He shook his head and drops of sweat sprayed away from his flesh. Josiah C. Hedges would have been concerned about that. The man called Edge didn't give a shit about it. What he did give a shit about was that four punk cowpunchers had beat the shit out of him and he was still suffering the effects of the beating. That had to be worth a thousand fucking bucks.

He yanked the door open and staggered into a

passage which ran from the rear to the front of the building where bright sunlight streamed in through a window. He peered along it with his eyes cracked against the brilliance and saw where the stairs ended halfway along on the right.

He should have used those stairs instead of taking all that time, using all that nervous energy, and suffering all that extra pain to get out through the window.

That had all been for nothing, too.

And why had he done it?

To keep clear of the Indians until he found his gear, the saddlebags with a couple of cartons of shells for the Winchester in them. He didn't want to be halfway down the stairs and meet some curious Comanche coming up when there were six of them armed with Winchesters. He just had an empty rifle and the Frontier Colt.

Why hadn't the bastards started putting Joe Straw to a slow death earlier? They'd gotten Edge riled up enough to hit them hard and fast right off instead of pussy-footing around looking for rifle shells he might not find until it was too late.

Damn the stupid questions that nobody was going to answer.

Straw was shrieking another high pitched and drawn out plea for his suffering to be at an end. Edge knew how he felt. He could smell the sickly stench of roasting flesh which negated the odors rising from his own body. He was sickly because he knew it was human meat that was cooking.

Another bottle smashed.

Evil delight was voiced by every Comanche brave.

The strange roar sounded again. This time

Edge recognized it for what it was as he staggered along the sunbright passage, Colt thrust ahead of him.

The noise of a great tongue of flame exploded from a fire when liquid fuel was splashed on it.

The victim's scream masked the shouts of his tormentors which covered the thud of Edge's footfalls along the passage.

He swung into the archway immediately across from the foot of the stairs and gazed across the width of the room into the contorted face of a man feeling greater agony than he did. He drew back his lips from clenched teeth to rasp, "Hi, you half-baked half-breed."

Chapter Thirteen

The white heat was taken out of Edge's anger and the powerful emotion was reduced to a tiny ball of ice in the pit of his stomach. It was no colder than the look in his glinting eyes as they made a lightning survey of the room.

The room that was almost a perfect replica of the one at Way Station Number Three, with Boston rockers by the front window, the counter along one side with a gap at the center to separate liquor from provision sales areas, and the trestle tables and bench seats at the rear.

The main difference was that, instead of a cooking range, this room had a corner fireplace, which was the instrument of Joe Straw's torture.

His wrists were lashed together again, but they were above his head now, the bonds hooked over a wall bracket which usually supported a kerosene lamp. The bracket was at such a height that with his arms fully extended, just the tips of his toes touched the hearth.

He was naked except for his spurred boots, his pants, and Indian waistcoat having been burned off him by the roaring flames of the fire in the grate behind him. Flames diminished as the last drops of liquor from the second bottle smashed against the rear of the fireplace were consumed.

Edge triggered a shot from the Colt and tracked the gun onto a new target without seeing the first bullet puncture the back of an Indian. He shot a second brave in the same area—midway between waist and shoulder, left of center—before the others were aware of his intrusion.

They were all grouped in front of the screaming and writhing Straw, intensely interested in the suffering of their victim until they saw two of their number fall, blood pumping from the back wounds.

They were not as drunk as Straw had been at the way station down the south trail, but more drunk than the cowpunchers and totally unprepared for the lethal trouble that had exploded upon them.

Edge shot a third Comanche while they were still staring at the first two who had not yet finished spasming on the floor. The bullet drilled into the left side of this one. His fall sent him crashing into Straw, who swung helplessly into the fire and screamed to the full extent of his vocal range as the flames licked his bare legs before he came forward and cleared them.

None of the Comanches had sidearms, just knives and tomahawks on their weapon belts. Each of them clutched a bottle of rye. Each had discarded his Winchester to have both hands free for eating, drinking, and torturing.

The cold anger that gripped Edge had a cooling effect on his thought processes. He was

172

able to see each important detail and catalogue it in terms of how it threatened his survival.

One brave dropped into a crouch as he whirled around, and reached for his knife. Edge blasted a shot into the top of his head.

Before this Comanche was knocked onto his rump and began toppling backwards, the other two were diving for rifles, one to the left and the other to the right.

Edge allied speed with deliberation to select his next target—the brave who had the least distance to get to a Winchester. He shot him in the side of the head, the bullet biting out a piece of his ear before drilling into his skull.

"Edge!" Joe Straw shrieked in terrified warning.

The Frontier Colt tracked from the sprawling brave, across the tortured form of the half-breed Comanche and drew a bead on the final target, who was stretched full-length on his side, a double-handed grip on a rifle which he had swung to aim at Edge. On the periphery of his vision, Edge had seen the brave work the lever action, but no shell or shellcase had been ejected.

The rifle trigger was squeezed and the expression of evil triumph was abruptly wiped from the emaciated face of the brave. Edge checked his own trigger finger, without putting warmth into the ice cold grin that had formed on his battered features when the slaughter began.

A hysterical laugh was forced from Straw's throat. "I knowed it! I knowed them sons of bitches had give me an empty rifle to hit this place! That's the one!"

The surviving brave was staring down in horror at the Winchester which had responded with a

173

dry click when he squeezed the trigger. He jerked his head to stare with malevolent defiance at the tall white man who moved between the gap in the counter.

"If there ain't no bullet, it can't have my name on it, feller," Edge said softly, and fired the final shot from the Colt. He placed it between the teeth and into the back of the throat as the Comanche gaped his mouth to voice a curse.

The brave died instantly and was jerked over onto his back, the wrench of his head causing a stream of blood to jet out in a whiplash action, and lay a stain from his mouth to the foot of the wall beside the fireplace.

Edge's nostrils were filled with the stench of his own sweat, the stale vomit, the rye whiskey spilled from the bottles dropped by dying braves, gunsmoke, and the scorched flesh of Joe Straw.

Waves of pain crashed over him again. The empty Winchester dropped from his left hand and the Colt which had been expended came free of his right. If he had not been standing between the two sections of the counter and able to support himself with a hand on the top of each, he would have fallen.

The corpse-littered scene swam before his eyes. He heard Straw say something to him, but lacked the ability to concentrate. His mind was concerned entirely with his own suffering, then he fastened on something outside—one of the stinks assaulting his nostrils.

The whiskey.

He backed painfully from between the gap, but needed to steady himself with one hand on the counter as he moved along it. He reached a fresh bottle of rye from a shelf, pulled out the cork with his teeth, and spat it to the floor. He raised the bottle and drank from it.

The liquor going down his throat met bile coming up, but he fought against gagging and won.

"Hey, man. Please cut me down, man."

Edge heard the weakly spoken words after he had taken a second drink from the bottle and the liquor got all the way into his stomach without resistance.

"It ain't midday yet," he muttered.

"What man?"

Edge was talking to himself. He turned and leaned his elbows on the counter, holding the bottle in both hands. "Medicinal." He raised his eyes from the bottle and gazed bleakly over at Straw.

Behind the almost totally naked man the fire was dying, and so was Joe Straw. When it had been stoked high, fueled with dry wood, exploded into roaring intensity by the whiskey, the flames must have seared terrible injuries across the back of the man after burning the clothing off him. Edge could see areas of his legs and flanks where the flesh was scorched black and marked with ugly blisters.

But it wasn't the burns he would die of.

"No, Joe."

"What?" Straw was weakened by a degree of agony far greater than that which Edge was experiencing. But he had the strength of will to keep his head from dropping forward and to shout the single word.

"The Indians roasted you, Joe, I need to grill you."

"Shit, man, you can't let me—"

"Seems to me I can do whatever I like."

"Go to hell!"

"Something I figure you know about, Joe."

He eased up from the counter and left the bottle where it was. Straw watched him in horror as he moved back along the counter, then was dumbstruck for long moments when he turned to go through the archway instead of coming out of the gap.

"Don't leave me here!" he wailed with a sob when Edge had gone from sight. "I'll tell you what you want if I can!"

Edge could hear him still sobbing until he was outside and across the yard.

The team which had hauled the Concord from Way Station Number Three was in the stable. So was the black mare with Edge and John Hackman's saddles and bedrolls.

He checked that the money was still in the saddlebag. He counted out eight hundred dollars from the bills Straw had stolen from the stagecoach in Colorado and pushed it into a shirt pocket.

He saddled the mare, lashed his bedroll in place, and led the animal through the doorway into the corral across to the gate that opened onto the trail and over to the stage, where he hitched the reins. Again he opened a saddlebag and this time took out a carton of shells. He carried the saddlebag in through the open doorway of the way station, without looking at the sprawled corpses of the father and son who used to run it.

He avoided even glancing at the dead because he was not yet ready to trust himself to control

176

the anger at their dying. To keep this feeling ice cold was the way of the man called Edge. He did not want yet to test that Josiah C. Hedges was really dead.

Straw jerked up his tear stained face and showed an expression of relief. "So you ain't gonna leave me here, man?"

Edge ignored him to cross to the gap between the two lengths of counter where he picked up his Colt and Winchester. This didn't hurt quite as much as when he had swung the saddle up across the back of the mare.

"Please, man . . ."

Edge kept his back to the naked man as he fed shells through the loading gate of the Winchester, then extracted the empty cartridge cases from the Colt and reloaded the chambers with fresh bullets from his gunbelt. He holstered the revolver and left the Winchester on the countertop as he went along behind the provisions side. He found some notepaper and a pencil which the father and son used to total the cost of purchases. He began to write.

"What are you doin', man?" Straw pleaded.

Edge finished writing the short message, folded the paper and left it on the counter. He took out the eight hundred dollars from his shirt pocket and placed it on top. Then he moved back where he had left the Winchester, canted it to his shoulder, and looked at Straw hanging helplessly from the wall bracket.

"Just idle curiosity, Joe," he said wearily. "But I figure the people on the stagecoach turned you loose or you made a run for it. You came by this place and saw the set-up ahead of the stage. It was fixed for me to be taken care of here and the stagecoach pulled out. You had a run-in with the bunch of renegade Comanches and talked them out of killing you by telling them—"

"I was headin' for Phoenix, man," Straw said eagerly. "They shot my horse out from under me. And they sure would've killed me. I had to think of somethin', so I told them about the stagecoach comin' through. It was slaughter, man. Them double crossin' Comanches been on the run from the army for days without nothin' to eat. They just closed in on that stagecoach and pumped lead into it. Killed everyone aboard.

"When I saw you wasn't aboard, I figured them people had left you out in the friggin' desert. Then I wasn't friggin' thinkin' about nothin' except stayin' alive again. On account of there was no grub on the stagecoach and they was itchin' to kill me for wastin' their time. So I thought up the idea about hittin' this place. You can't blame me for that, man. Shit, if your life was on the friggin' line, I bet you'd to anythin' to save your neck."

"Obliged, Joe."

He advanced on the half-breed Comanche with the dead braves sprawled on the floor around his dangling form.

"Edge, for God's sake man! What you gonna do? What's with the letter and the money?" He swallowed hard. "You ain't gonna . . . ?"

Edge moved an outstretched arm of one of the dead with the toe of his boot and came to a halt in front of Straw.

"I never let a favor go unreturned, Joe. And I always expect to be paid what I'm owed."

178

Another sob burst from Straw's trembling lips. "What about John Hackman? If I ain't taken back to Crater and hung he got his for nothin', man! And you ain't no cold-blooded killer!"

The green eyes in the Indian face under the red hair pleaded for mercy.

"That was another feller, Joe. He's dead now."

"What?"

"I was a little confused myself," Edge said flatly. "Right up to the time when these Indians started in to kill you slow, Joe. And the feller I used to be got mad enough to bring me running in here with just a six-shooter. Up against six Comanches."

"Please, Edge?" Straw groaned.

"That's who I am, Joe. And that's who those people on the stage and the two fellers who ran this place took care of while I couldn't help myself. And you got all of them killed. They won't know I'm returning the favor, but I will.

"And the eight hundred dollars on the counter over there is what you stole, less the thousand reward. The letter explains that to whoever finds you here, Joe. It asks that the eight hundred dollars be sent back to Crater. Along with word that you're dead."

Straw allowed the gaze of his tear-filled eyes to fall to the corpse-littered floor in front of him. And he spoke venomously.

"You're the worst kind of bastard there is, man. You waited until these stinkin' Indians had given me some of their kinda hell before you made your move, didn't you? Got my hopes way up high that I was gonna be okay. Now you're gonna finish me.

179

I tell you what I wish, man. I wish you hadn't come through that arch and given me hope!"

Now he raised his gaze to stare into the narrowed eyes of Edge.

"It has to be me, Joe. Or I couldn't return the favors or claim the reward. And look on the bright side." He drew the razor from the neck pouch and the sunlight danced on the honed blade.

"Oh, dear God," Straw breathed, barely audible.

"I can fix a flesh wound, Joe. The kind of burns you have, I can't take care of. So it would be a painful ride up to Crater. Hurt you as much, maybe, as the Indians were hurting you. And then, at the end of it, you'd be hanged."

The half-breed Comanche injected an expression of depthless hatred into his eyes as he kept his gaze locked on that of Edge.

"So do it, you bastard!" he snarled. "Don't try and tell me how friggin' lucky I am, you Mex greaser. The worst kind of lousy friggin' bas—"

It caused Edge a great deal of pain to move his arm with such speed, bringing it up from his side and then slashing it across so that the razor fisted in his hand opened up a deep wound in the throat of Joe Straw from an inch below the right ear to an identical point under the left one. He withdrew his hand with equal speed, so that none of the blood that gushed from the massive wound splashed him.

Straw jerked for a few seconds while a series of choked sounds were forced up through the blood in his severed throat. Then he became totally limp.

Edge wiped the razor on the curly hair of the

dead man and pushed it back into the neck pouch. He went toward the open doorway with the morning sunlight streaming through it. He halted on the threshold and, despite the pain without anguish that assaulted him, he spread a cold grin across his bruised face as he turned for a final glance at the corpse sagging in the fireplace.

"To you I was everything you said, Joe," he drawled softly. "But ain't no denying that for awhile toward the end, you warmed to me."

EDGE
BY
George G. Gilman

More bestselling western adventure from Pinnacle, America's #1 series publisher. Over 8 million copies of EDGE in print!

the EXECUTIONER by Don Pendleton

Relax...and enjoy more of America's #1 bestselling action/adventure series! Over 25 million copies in print!

- ☐ 41-065-4 War Against The Mafia #1 $2.25
- ☐ 41-714-4 Death Squad #2 $2.25
- ☐ 41-669-7 Battle Mask #3 $2.25
- ☐ 41-823-X Miami Massacre #4 $2.25
- ☐ 41-069-7 Continental Contract #5 $1.95
- ☐ 41-831-0 Assault On Soho #6 $2.25
- ☐ 41-071-9 Nightmare In New York #7 $1.95
- ☐ 41-763-2 Chicago Wipeout #8 $2.25
- ☐ 41-073-5 Vegas Vendetta #9 $1.95
- ☐ 41-074-3 Caribbean Kill #10 $1.95
- ☐ 41-832-9 California Hit #11 $2.25
- ☐ 41-833-7 Boston Blitz #12 $2.25
- ☐ 41-855-8 Washington I.O.U. #13 $2.25
- ☐ 41-078-6 San Diego Siege #14 $1.95
- ☐ 41-079-4 Panic In Philly #15 $1.95
- ☐ 41-080-8 Sicilian Slaughter #16 $1.95
- ☐ 41-882-5 Jersey Guns #17 $2.25
- ☐ 41-764-0 Texas Storm #18 $2.25
- ☐ 41-830-2 Detroit Deathwatch #19 $2.25
- ☐ 41-853-1 New Orleans Knockout #20 $2.25

- ☐ 40-757-2 Firebase Seattle #21 $1.75
- ☐ 41-086-7 Hawaiian Hellground #22 $1.95
- ☐ 40-759-9 St. Louis Showdown #23 $1.75
- ☐ 40-760-2 Canadian Crisis #24 $1.75
- ☐ 41-089-1 Colorado Kill-Zone #25 $1.95
- ☐ 41-090-5 Acapulco Rampage #26 $1.95
- ☐ 41-091-3 Dixie Convoy #27 $1.95
- ☐ 41-092-1 Savage Fire #28 $1.95
- ☐ 40-765-3 Command Strike #29 $1.75
- ☐ 41-094-8 Cleveland Pipeline #30 $1.95
- ☐ 41-095-6 Arizona Ambush #31 $1.95
- ☐ 41-096-4 Tennessee Smash #32 $1.95
- ☐ 41-815-9 Monday's Mob #33 $2.25
- ☐ 41-765-9 Terrible Tuesday #34 $2.25
- ☐ 41-801-9 Wednesday's Wrath #35 $2.25
- ☐ 41-854-X Thermal Thursday #36 $2.25
- ☐ 41-883-3 Friday's Feast #37 $2.25
- ☐ 41-796-9 Satan's Sabbath #38 $2.25
- ☐ 41-700-4 Executioner Trilogy: The Beginning (trade size) $5.95

Buy them at your local bookstore or use this handy coupon
Clip and mail this page with your order

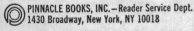

PINNACLE BOOKS, INC. — Reader Service Dept.
1430 Broadway, New York, NY 10018

Please send me the book(s) I have checked above. I am enclosing $_____ (please add 75¢ to cover postage and handling). Send check or money order only—no cash or C.O.D.'s.

Mr./Mrs./Miss _____

Address _____

City _____ State/Zip _____

Please allow six weeks for delivery. Prices subject to change without notice.